1959 Rome, Vatican City

*The Secret of Fatima has been placed
in one of those archives which are like a very deep,
dark well, to the bottom of which papers fall and
are never seen again.*

THE HOLY INQUISITION PREFECT,
CARDINAL ALFREDO OTTAVIANI

*Indeed, indeed listen to the very significant story
in these books by Raechel Sands ....
In wanting to endorse this work, a remarkable line
of Hafiz comes to mind. That verse goes:*

*I am a hole in a flute that the Christ's breath
moves through – listen to this music*

DANIEL LADINSKY, INTERNATIONALLY ACCLAIMED PENGUIN BOOKS
POET AND TRANSLATOR

THE

HIDING GAME

SAGA

TIGER

ROMEO

METAPOX

———————

#1

Advance
Review Copy

uncorrected proof =

r a e c h e l   s a n d s

Tiger Romeo is an imprint of Goldheart Ltd a UK company - www.goldheart.gold

Published by Tiger Romeo 2017
First published in paperback in 2017 by Tiger Romeo
First published in Great Britain, the United States and Australia
in 2017 by Tiger Romeo

Copyright © Goldheart Ltd 2017

Raechel Sands is represented by Nancy Owen Barton Agency - nowenb@aol.com

Raechel Sands asserts the moral right to be identified as the author of this work

FATIMA SECRET 1917 – 2017 CENTENARY EDITION

Cover and book design by Keith Sheridan
Cover photograph by Paolo De Faveri

Page 166 contains a list of writers whose works have been cited in this book

A catalogue record of this book is available at the British Library

ISBN 978 1 912148 00 4

CONTENTS

P ROLOGUE ≥ 7

M ETAPOX #1

1959 Cape Cod, USA

*No names have been changed to protect the innocent,
since God Almighty protects the innocent
as a matter of Heavenly routine.*

KURT VONNEGUT JR.

Genghis Khan's army

*physically slaughtered some 40 million people, but his
invasion of the Crimea should be recognized as
the most spectacular incident of germ warfare in history,
with the the Black Death as its disastrous
consequence. The world population did not recover to
pre-plague levels for over three hundred years.*

CENTERS FOR DISEASE CONTROL AND PREVENTION (CDC)
EMERGING INFECTIOUS DISEASES, VOLUME 8, NO.9

PROLOGUE

She's Not There

O Reader, let us not turn our faces from the truth of History. Although She is ragged, hurried and confused, care-worn with the pain of countless human beings — is not the face of History ultimately beautiful?

If you will ... imagine mountains ... the Dinaric Alps of South eastern Europe, and the cold light before the dawn.

A pair of brown-and-white goats with large inscrutable eyes watch as damp soil flies through the thin air. Another shovelful flies from a spade, held in the hands of a girl. The rays of the rising sun strike the girl's face, catching a look of grief. With the back of her hand she wipes a tear from her cheek, smudging it with mud. She starts shovelling again.

Finally her task is done. All that remains is a few handfuls of earth. The girl sits and rests her hands on the handle. Her hands, face and hair are dark brown. But the hairs on her arms stand out in their blondness, as do her piercing Slavic blue eyes.

Slight and distinctive – if she were not so care-worn her face would have been *praised for its beauty.*

She should have been a young woman entering the prime of her life. Instead she is burying a body. A dead person. One corpse – a mere drop in the ocean of History.

*T*he girl does not know what the Red Army reported seventy years earlier when they liberated Auschwitz. In the years that followed voices rose, claiming to be voices of history, and declared the genocide of the Holocaust 'made up', and our politicians allowed those voices to do what they have always done: *bury the truth.*

But the girl has one scene from her childhood etched in her mind. Her paternal grandmother, who taught her English and had been a history and piano teacher before the Bosnian War, was pounding on a derelict piano in the basement of a café bombed out in the War. The sound, coming from her always-gentle Grandmother terrified her; it was unbearably loud and harsh. 'Listen,' Grandmother shouted. 'Listen to the cacophony of history, the shouting match of lies! The Nazi's Final Solution, their *big idea,* their grand symphonic butchery! went to Number One in 1942 with the iconic *I Wannakill Conference*,' she yelled, over the cacophony she was making on the piano.

'But trying to gas the eleven million Jews of Europe was not enough, they wanted another guaranteed hit. So they came up with *Generalplan Ost.* A catchy little number. Do you know what it was? It was to eliminate people like you and me, darling my dear.' The girl had started crying but still Grandmother did not stop thumping the piano keys. 'They had *vast prairies* planned for Eastern Europe, and their kill list was the three hundred million Slavs who lived there. Here in our tiny Bosniak nation, they only managed to murder one hundred and ten thousand: how disappointed they must have been!'

The girl was sobbing now. Her Grandmother stopped pounding, played one last soulful, major chord, and took the girl in her arms.

'But what of the Allies?' she whispered. 'Our *heroes*? The British and Commonwealth forces, the Americans, the Russians. What did they do?'

Her mother's face was gentle again. She even smiled.

'They composed a coda: a final requiem for the Third Reich they said. *It was over.* And they told us to go home.'

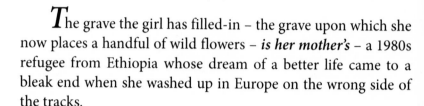

*T*he grave the girl has filled-in – the grave upon which she now places a handful of wild flowers – *is her mother's* – a 1980s refugee from Ethiopia whose dream of a better life came to a bleak end when she washed up in Europe on the wrong side of the tracks.

The bells of a distant church start ringing and are joined by the bells of a second, nearer church. Like her late father, the girl is an indigenous European Muslim and she does not wear a headscarf. The bells mean it is the day Christians call Easter Sunday: the day Jesus Christ rose from the grave. The Qur'an says that Jesus, Son of Mary, will return at the end of the world. Maybe that's when the meek will inherit the earth, the girl thinks. Some hope. But today the world did not come to an end: just the day she buried her mother.

She bites her lip and swallows her tears. At this moment in her grief she must hold on to something. She can no longer hold and kiss her own mother, so she kneels and kisses the mother goat Cassandra.

The girl's name is **Leila**, Leila Muhic.

She's nineteen years old and this is what she knows from her Grandmother. The dreams of her black mother, Fatima Muhic, had turned to nightmares. Leila's mother and father were peasant farmers in a mountain village called Liplje. They had very little but somehow survived the freezing winter of 1994-5 as the Bosnian War raged around them. They were pleased when Fatima fell pregnant for the first time, with Leila. But only for a short while, because they were made prisoners as their village was turned into a modern-day concentration camp.

Leila's father was executed, and Fatima systematically raped, despite being pregnant. As spring changed to summer, Leila grew big inside Fatima's womb and the concentration camp was liberated. The foreign sun softened, the hard mountains cooled and darkened, the Earth entered the sign of Libra – the Scales of Justice – and *Leila was born.*

President Bill Clinton's Dayton Accord, her grandmother had explained, brought an end to the rape and killing. But the murderers had won the Hiding Game. There was a blank on the map of Europe. The village of Liplje was no more.

⭐

Grandmother, Fatima and Leila got as far from Zvornik District as they could. Although left alive, Fatima was also gone, gone in spirit. She accepted guidance, ate, slept and went to the toilet, but she didn't smile or speak. . Her eyes were vacant and, except for a constant anxiety that only found voice at night in sudden fits, she was lost to the world. 'If only she would scream,' Grandmother said, 'Maybe she could talk once more. Maybe she could somehow return to herself.'

Fatima was diagnosed with TB that was too far gone to cure. After Grandmother died, Leila bravely nursed her silent mother alone. When the final illness came, there was a new animation in Fatima's eyes as if to say: This I can fight, this will destroy me but I can fight it. On her death bed she gripped Leila's hand and uttered a few faltering words. In death the relentlessly open eyes were at last quiet.

Leila was on her own, without even the money for a bus fare. In school her science teacher said she showed great potential, if only she came more often. But the girl was fierce only in her determination to learn about the world – 'the world of goodness beyond the mountains of fear,' she called it. She would leave the Balkans and go to her only relative, her mother's brother in Berlin; or to America, maybe to the Dayton Ohio her Grandmother had talked about. The moon, setting in the mountains towards Croatia, marked the way. Leila had come of age.

*S*tanding over the grave, Leila says, '*Tamo, to je gotovo.*' Then tells herself she must think and talk in English, not Bosniak-Serbo-Croat. 'There, that's done,' she says.

Her only possessions are her two goats, a few things in her knapsack (including a lightweight tent, a smart phone and a journal that she writes poetry in) and her encyclopaedic knowledge of rock songs. She wipes the brown earth from her hands onto a rag, puts the rag in the pocket of her worn out yellow dress, and kneels once more at the grave. She says the final part of the Salāt al-Janāzah and the Muslim words for parting, then '*Allah Akbar,*' and gets up. 'I hope to meet you again in heaven,' she says to her mother. '*Onda ćemo razgovarati.* We will talk then. *Inshallah.*'
Turning to the goats, Leila unties them, tilts her head quizzically and says, '*Idemo.* Come on then.' She takes Cassandra's tether, slings her knapsack over her shoulder and climbs a trail for half a mile, Cassandra's kid trotting behind.

The Easter bells are ringing tirelessly now. By a meadow of buttercups above the graveyard Leila stops and surveys her old life. The goats look too, and then nuzzle her. She sinks down into the wild flowers, opens the knapsack and takes out some Bosniac sweet bread for herself and some horse chestnuts for the goats. After their snack, the goats watch as Leila rolls through the buttercups, smiling as the petals caress her face, covering it and the skin of her bare legs in yellow pollen.

A harmonica tumbles from her pocket, a birthday gift from the uncle. An American forces chaplain had taught her to play it. He'd liked a singer named Neil Young and his song *Heart of Gold* goes through her head now.

Getting up from the buttercups she looks at her legs and – for the first time in months – *laughs*. She twirls around, her arms raised high to the sky, and laughs at the top of her voice.

The Nubian goats look relieved when Leila falls over. Crawling to her knapsack, she powers up her Noa phone, opens the Maps Pro app and checks her route through the limestone mountains. She blows through the harmonica (a Hohner) to clear the keys, removes the tether from Cassandra and marches north along a footpath into the pine forest. Cassandra and kid trot behind. When they look up expectantly, she says to them in good English, 'Here's a little song I know', puts the Hohner to her lips, and starts playing an Elton John track called *Where To Now St. Peter?*

> *Dirty was the daybreak*
> *Sudden was the change*
> *In such a silent place as this*
> *Beyond the rifle range* [1]

Cupping her hands around her mouth, she yells through the mountains at the top of her voice.
'Rock'n'roll will never die.'
'Never die,' comes back the echo.
Suddenly giddy again, she dances around her goats then turns and shouts to the mountains:
'My name's Leila. Leila Muhic! And I will change the world!'

Exactly one thousand miles to the Northwest, on London's orbital motorway (the M25) sat an American heiress twice the age of Leila and with a curious nickname: Blanka.

Blanka (christened *Boudica Valentina Maguire*) was alone in the back of a red taxi cab, crawling through thick London fog towards Heathrow Airport. The neon lights shimmered unnaturally, thought Blanka. At Leila's age she had also lost her mother and, like Leila, just recently death had beset her again. On her left arm she wore a black armband. She was a Christian, a Roman Catholic. Not so much a lapsed one as a worn-out one, but she played with the blood red Rosary beads that dangled from her wrist all the same.

In her public life Blanka was known for her philanthropy and her devotion to the conservation and protection of wildlife, and for her success as a guitarist and DJ on the music scene. Unknown to the public, she was also a high-ranking Intelligence officer in the CIA and NATO, with the codename Ʊ4 (OhZone 4).

A brake light screamed – and Blanka gaped as a drop of blood appeared before her and fell to the floor of the cab. She stared at it and caught her breath, 'Fuck, not now.'
'Alright darling?' the cabbie asked over the microphone, breaking the spell. 'Can you believe this weather? Sure your flight'll be going?'
Blanka blinked and looked at the floor again. The blood had gone, magically absolved. 'It's a private jet,' she said, 'special clearance.'

The jet waiting for her belonged to Professor Max Hart her stepfather, and his collaborator Dr Oxberry. She'd received a transatlantic call from her stepfather only shortly before. His son, her half-brother Will (William P. Hart) had locked himself into the 'History Lab' at his private school and was refusing to come out. That information, though it angered her stepfather, only amused Blanka.

The History Lab was the nickname the pupils had given to the $20m state-of-the-art archaeological training tool Hart had donated to the school at Croton-on-Hudson, just outside New York City. At a computer terminal in one of the fieldwork areas, Will had constantly typed and re-typed possible solutions to the un-deciphered Bronze Age inscription dubbed 'Linear G' adorning the outside of Hart and Oxberry's archaeological master-work – *The Goldheart.*

Another piece of information had compelled Blanka to begin her journey to New York immediately.

Will could also be heard repeating, over and over, the lines of a song – a song Blanka knew well. It was part of the repertoire of *Point Blanka,* the band she and Will had formed with Sokol Comarova, another woman Intelligence agent. As the cab pulled into one of Heathrow's special security areas, Blanka hummed it to herself

> *Well, no one told me about her*
> *The way she lied*
> *Well, no one told me about her*
> *How many people cried*
>
> *But it's too late to say you're sorry*
> *How would I know? Why should I care?*
> *Please don't bother trying to find her*
> *She's not there* [2]

Hart had driven Will home to their loft in the Garment District, and it was there that Blanka headed when her jet landed at La Guardia. After a chat with her stepfather, she approached her half-brother's bedroom, bearing gifts she knew he would appreciate: a 'diplomatic pouch' containing MI6 headed notepaper and an original vinyl copy of Black Sabbath's *Master of Reality.*

When she opened the door to his soundproofed room, the muffled drumming from inside became deafening thunder. Will sat at his drum kit, behind a base drum emblazoned with the name *Point Blanka*. He beamed at Blanka, set down his sticks, and removed his headphones. 'Hi, Sis.'

'I expected to find you comatose,' she laughed, 'but I don't think I've ever seen you looking so well.'

'Everybody thinks I'm nuts.'

'Are you?'

'No more than usual.'

Taking her time, Blanka slumped into the swivel chair in front of a bronze chessboard with gold and silver pieces arranged on it. She studied the board for a moment. 'This is new. Looks like you're set up for a game.'

'Dad wants me to learn.'

'The pieces are a little off. You've got the gold king and queen reversed. The queen should be on the darker square.' As she spoke, Blanka switched them.

'Dad says the queen has all the power,' commented Will.

'How about one of these?' She picked up a gold pawn and waved it. 'Don't they have any power?'

'Not much.'

'They do if they move six squares to the end of the board.' Blanka paused, Will wasn't listening. 'So what's really going on?' she asked as casually as possible.

'She's back, Blanka!' Will exclaimed, suddenly animated. 'She's *come back.*'

The gold pawn Blanka held fell to the floor and rolled around with its own momentum. She watched it rolling then picked it up. Is it true? she thought. *His* truth, but is it *the* truth? Could she have come back? I suppose if we believe it's a magical world, anything's possible. And what happens if she has?

She looked at Will and blinked, taking in the magnitude of his revelation. Her eyes filled with a soft glow, as of candlelight. 'This calls for a celebration.' She placed the pawn on the board, got up from the chair and hugged him. She took a bag of Lindor dark chocolate balls from her turquoise eco-friendly handbag, and dished out three each.

'Essentials,' she said.

'Essentials,' Will agreed. Blanka smiled, unwrapped the chocolate balls, popped one into her mouth and another into her brother's.

'Then, where is – *she*?' Blanka asked.

'Close. I can feel her getting closer,' he said. 'I think she's heading for The Goldheart. When she comes, we can finally decipher the inscription.'

In the awkward way teenagers sometimes have, Will suddenly changed the subject. 'Look at this. I've been watching it a lot lately.' Moving to his keyboard, he brought up a YouTube video of the song Blanka had hummed in the taxi. The Zombies' 1964 hit, *She's Not There*. Sitting next to each other, they watched the video and sang softly

> *Well, let me tell you 'bout the way she looked*
> *The way she acts and the color of her hair*
> *Her voice was soft and cool*
> *Her eyes were clear and bright*
> *But she's not there* [2]

Blanka looked at her brother intently. He felt the look and turned sombre. 'If she's here, I'll find her for you,' Blanka said. 'But you have to go back to school tomorrow and behave normally.'

'Fifteen-year-olds aren't supposed to be normal.'

'I still want you to go back to school. Try not to attract so much attention.'

*B*efore she left the loft Blanka went into her stepfather's study. Hart was at the bar behind his grand piano, mixing another of the White Russian cocktails with which he punctuated his day.

'He wants to keep watch on The Goldheart,' said Blanka.

Hart snorted and shook his head. 'Does he expect her to pop out of it? I dug it up from *the seabed,* I can tell you what's inside – heavy, precious gold. It's made us all very rich. *She's not there.*'

'I don't think he means it literally. He thinks she'll try to reach it.'

'He can't spend his time staking it out.'

'You're a trustee of the Met, he can hang out there all he likes.' Then she added, 'By the way, he doesn't like chess.'

Hart knocked back half the White Canadian (Kahlúa, Vodka and goats milk). 'It helps you think. More thinking, less feeling.'

He savoured the taste. 'Now when are we going to find an OhZone who's an "A" positive organ match for your kidney?'

'Hans is in The Machine now.'

'Good try,' said Hart sarcastically, 'But he's "A" negative.'

'After everything that's happened, it's the least of our problems.'

'I disagree,' Hart persisted.

'What does your hero say? *Every little thing will be alright.* Let's get William Paris Hart sorted out first.'

'You can't believe this stuff,' *said Hart. 'It's childish nonsense.*'

'If and when she gets here... I'll find her, then he'll be proved right.' She smiled.

Hart shook his head. He could see the spirit of Will and Blanka's long-dead mother – Kitty Maguire – simultaneously fearless feisty and foolhardy – in her daughter's face.

He could never prevail against Kitty's logic and he could not prevail against her daughter ☡

Darling my dear
    I tell you what is right
        The moon on the lake
            And swimming by its light

        Darling my dear
            I tell you what is wrong
                I went to the mountain
                    But the mountain top was gone [3]

 LISSIE - BACK TO FOREVER

Cumming? What Is In A Name?

To understand God's thoughts we must study statistics for these are the measure of his purpose [4]

FLORENCE NIGHTINGALE - CITED IN CHANCE RULES :
AN INFORMAL GUIDE TO PROBABILITY

Four Years Earlier: February 25, 2011

Vale of White Horse District, Oxfordshire, United Kingdom

*I*n the normal world, Blanka dedicated her life and fortune to the protection of wild animals. In the world of espionage, she had started at nineteen because of her grandfather, US Admiral William Maguire, and now she was a force to be reckoned with. She was currently stationed, next to the Russia Desk, on the twelfth floor of the London headquarters of British Military Intelligence Section 6.

Misinformation, dissembling and a certain vagueness were the bread-and-butter of Intelligence. Even the names of the highest officials suffered from the side effects. Since 1911 the head of MI6 had been known simply as 'C,' after its eccentric one-legged founder and ladies' man, Mansfield Cumming. A pioneer of the sword-stick as lethal weapon and his agents' semen as invisible ink, the original 'C' was also the man behind the murder of the famous Russian monk, Grigori Rasputin.

The present long-standing and more openly sexual head of MI6, the current 'C,' Sir Tony Sharp, carried on the tradition and always referred to 'his' organization by its codename *The Office*. Staff who were younger and more forward-thinking compensated by assigning clever names, as opposed to vague and stupid ones. C's protégé and lover, Marcia Miles (nicknamed 'Bio' by her boss in Science Division) had quickly tagged Blanka, 'Queen Boudica,' and MI6 itself, *Wonderland* – as it came to be known throughout the Intelligence world.

Well, as Blanka herself would admit, if a name was good, it stuck to you like shit. And she in turn christened Bio, 'Queen Marcia.' The two celtic queens ruled their respective kingdoms (Science Division and OhZone) and developed a mutual respect. Another name that had stuck (even at CIA headquarters in Langley, Virginia) was *Ma Baker*, a name from Blanka's vinyl sampling pastime, which she had given the CIA chief at the London bureau (169 Baker Street N.W.1). The CIA Director (and Blanka's long-time mentor) enjoyed the fun. In official documents he referred to the subsequent CIA chiefs in London as 'Ma Baker,' which was no small annoyance to the men who had succeeded the original woman.

C answered (in theory) to the Foreign Secretary: the minister in charge of the Foreign and Commonwealth Office (the equivalent of the State Department). When Lucien Barker Johnson was promoted to the post, Blanka was quick to dub him, *L.B.J.*, after the American who took office after President Kennedy (J.F.K.) was murdered.

*O*ne woman at MI6 was known by an adjective that was also an adverb – 'Nearby'. Blanka first met her on a country lane west of Oxford. An MI6 blue-slip hit had been bungled. The target, a man, had been hideously wounded when electrocuted with a B&Q hedge trimmer. It was difficult to make the killing look like suicide or an accident. But Blanka wasn't concerned with the details of what to make it look like, she wanted the truth. Whatever lies were sold to the public, it was important to know the truth hiding underneath. When she arrived the clean-up squad had departed, leaving a handful of agents disguised as regular British bobbies. Behind the garden and up a tree, she had found a young woman perched, *Nearby*. She had not been detected earlier and when she came down she wouldn't say a word.

The silent woman seemed unworldly and was obviously frightened, but there was also a slow steadiness in her. When Blanka sat down to question her, *Nearby* just stared at her hands for ten minutes. Recognizing a pendant of St. Francis of Assisi around her neck, Blanka decided to try a more personal approach.
'I was brought up in a Catholic convent,' she said. 'You remind me of my best friend there, a girl called Bridget.'
'I went to con-v-vent school,' Nearby stuttered in a Dublin accent, looking at the armed agents watching her. 'I wish I was there now.'
'Me too sometimes' Blanka said. 'But we can't stay in a convent all our lives. Did I mention that it was Bridget who taught me how to swear?'
'I don't swear,' Nearby giggled. 'At least I d-don't think I do.'
Although Blanka soon learned Nearby's real name, she left it buried in her file. As an eyewitness to the hit, several solutions were offered to the 'Nearby problem' (some more bloody than others). Blanka wanted to protect her and with perseverance she won out. Nearby was duly screened, tested and recruited to MI6, and she and Blanka went on to become close friends. C quipped at Nearby's swearing-in ceremony, 'Keep your friends close but your enemies nearby.'

On Blanka's recommendation Nearby became a loyal and dependable member of the Russia Desk. With an astounding talent for Russian, within three years she rose through its ranks to become the chief Russian-speaking liaison officer on the Desk.

As leader of NATO's elite *OhZone* agents (abbreviated ℧), Blanka was pleased when Russia Desk director Phil York, 'Russia,' proposed Nearby to replace the French agent ℧2 (OhZone 2) who had been killed in action. Only six candidates had ever passed through the half a billion dollars a pop, four month program of bio-engineering and training at the OhZone laboratory, so competition was stiff. But shifting office politics was also a consideration. During the illness of OhZone's chief sponsor, CIA Director Admiral De Leon, C had manoeuvred the European allies so that his latest protégé, nickname Felicity-fast-track, was prepped as an alternative. She was attached to the Latin American Desk and was jealous of Nearby and her bureau position on the top floor of headquarters. Not since Cain and Abel were there two humans more different in temperament than Felicity and Nearby; but in appearance they looked as alike as two peas in a pod.

One evening Blanka had taken Nearby to the nightclub where she DJ'd twice a month. Nearby confessed that in her three years at MI6 she'd been propositioned over fifty times by male agents, mistaking her for Felicity and wanting to get laid. As they danced to one of Blanka's surrealist favourites, she sang the title line to Nearby, 'What does the fox say?' followed by, 'And...?'
Nearby remaining characteristically silent. Blanka took her arms and spun her around and off the dance floor.
'You can tell me in Morse,' Blanka sang, 'I'll keep it secret of course. *What does the fox say?* [5]'

Nearby laughed. 'Alright,' she said, 'maybe the two or three who spoke Russian. Put me down!'

Blanka lowered Nearby, stopped dancing and stared at her. Nearby stared back. 'Don't be using your X-ray eyes on me now.'

'Russian?' continued Blanka. 'Russian! You fucked Andre Petrov, our captured Russian spy?'

Nearby mimicked surprise and whispered, 'If I told you, I'd have to kill you.'

'No wonder he melted like chocolate. You of all people, following along in Mansfield Cumming's footsteps!' Blanka said shaking her head. 'Never underestimate the quiet ones.'

*O*hZones were given their numbers in order of graduation

ROME ♅ PIONEER GROUP

♅1 ♂ DESERTED & OFF-THE-GRID ♅3 ♂ CRUSOE ROBINSON
♅2 ♂ DECEASED ♅4 ♀ BLANKA MAGUIRE

PARIS ♅ OHZONE LAB REBUILD

♅5 ♀ SOKOL COMAROVA ♅6 ♂ ON PATERNITY LEAVE

Now it was time to allocate ♅7. The candidates were vetted in several ways, including the eight-point CCU. One of Hart and Oxberry's inventions, it predicted psychopathic tendencies by tests, a psychopathy checklist and PET/MRI scans of the pre-frontal cortex. It correlated with those convicted of serial killing, ethnic cleansing and torture. Every individual scored as an 8 (extreme psychopath) was found to possess the CDH13 and MAOA-L 'psychopath' recessive gene-pairing. When Hart was asked in an interview with the *Journal of Evolutionary Biology* about CCU, he said, 'It quantifies how poorly *Homo sapiens* actually rate as the compassionate caring species we like to pretend we are.'

Felicity's score of 8 threatened her application, as did Nearby's unusual score of 1 (zero). At the last minute C had overridden computer security and altered Felicity's test result to a perfect 4.

Because Nearby had never raised a hand in violence, the defining issue became whether she would kill. A hearing into her pacifism was arranged before three MI6 directors: C, Russia and Bio (now newly promoted to director). Professor Hart flew from New York to attend as an observer alongside Blanka. She and Hart watched as Russia started, and Nearby responded with her usual directness.
'Are you loyal to Queen Elizabeth and to The Office?' he asked.
'I am,' Nearby answered.
'When you've been "firearms trained," will you shoot to kill if ordered to?' Russia asked. Nearby looked at Blanka.
C glared at them and barked, 'When you're all alone, without Queen Boudica to protect you, will you do as you're ordered to?'
Nearby had tears in her eyes. Russia repeated the question slowly. At first Nearby was silent and then she whispered to Russia, 'Shooting at a t-target... it's not the same as shooting at a hu-hu-human.'
Russia, deeply disappointed, frowned and turned to Blanka.
'But if you were ordered to do it?' Bio interjected.
Nearby was shaking. 'I-I-I'm not sure. It w-wouldn't be easy for me.'
C had laughed in Nearby's face, 'Not sure! Wouldn't be easy! You've got to sweat at Intelligence my girl, and follow orders to the letter.'

When it was announced that Felicity would become Ʊ7, a joke quickly made the rounds: 'They didn't ask Felicity if she would kill when ordered to. They asked her if she would *stop* killing when ordered to.'
For over a year, Nearby had shared a shower room with Felicity at the MI6 spy hostel on the Edgware Road, W.2 (how kind of Queen Elizabeth, thought Nearby, to provide a hostel for the junior spies of her realm). Felicity's small swastika tattoo was discretely concealed in a larger one, but the anthem of anti-Semitism was there

all the same. When C's fast-track protégé moved out of the hostel to her own house in S.W.12, suddenly able to afford the mortgage, it was no surprise. Nearby had overheard Felicity say to 'Prosthetics John' (of the MI6 prosthetics laboratory) that she would 'sort out' the black couple living next door there, if they annoyed her.

Later at Blanka's house, over a cup of one of Blanka's unique tea blends, Nearby explained to her and Hart what had gone wrong at the hearing. 'I felt sick. Debbie had told me a-b-bout what the junior girls call, *Sp-special-C*. C had done cunni-l-lingus, with rice paper inside Debbie, the day before in his private dining room, with his butler on guard outside the door. I wanted to quit Wonder-l-land.'
Blanka put her arm around Nearby. That dick-shit still at his sexual harassment. Did he offer her promotion?' Nearby nodded. 'Debbie must report it to Dr Fox. C should be canned.'
Much to Nearby's relief, Hart, having had a couple of White Canadians [a cocktail] turned the conversation to the more esoteric question of whether human canines were the mark of Cain and singled humans out as killers. The Professor revealed that men had the smallest canines of any male ape. And that this reflected reduced dimorphism between the sexes.
'Women will rule the world,' Blanka had commented.
'Yes, but *which k-kind of women?*' Nearby had countered.

In Nearby's soul the realization constantly haunted her that her failure – which unleashed Felicity as an OhZone – could jeopardize Blanka's life.
'What w-was it Kurt Vonne-g-gut said?' she blurted out as she finished her tea. 'If there are such things as angels, I hope that they are armed with A K-K-47s? Was that it? Alright, if there's nothing else for it, I'll learn to fire a gun.'
From that day on Hart looked on Nearby with a new respect. Blanka continued to puzzle over the hidden depths in the silent woman who she had found perched in a tree at the site of a botched killing

1.2

Monday, June 20, 2011
Zoologischer Garten, District 7, Zürich, Switzerland

*I*n early summer, Blanka Maguire's interest in animal conservation had taken her to a conference in Zürich which Diana Grinin, Assistant Curator of Mammals at Moscow Zoo was also attending. She was the young wife of Major Grigori Grinin, famous as a Nobel Laureate Russian scientist and Chess Grand Master. Blanka also knew him as an old friend of the Russian side of her mother's family. Despite the obvious political complications, she was proud of her relation to Valentina Starikova, who had been the first woman in space. Valentina's father was brother to Blanka's great grandmother, Lara Brown (née Starikova).

Blanka knew of Grinin in relation to the Starikovas because of what her stepfather had told her – and the relation was a painful one. In 1999 her mother Kitty Maguire had gone to Moscow to further her research into a film she was producing about the *Third Secret of Fatima*. As a relative of Kitty's grandmother, Valentina introduced Kitty to Grinin, who came from a St. Petersburg family that had raised Russian priests for generations. Grinin had taken Kitty to them in St. Petersburg, and their help had enabled her to solve the mystery of the Fatima Secret. Subsequently he had saved her life during a murder attempt on the bank of the River Neva. Unfortunately, he hadn't been able to prevent another attempt in Rome that had resulted in Kitty's death.

On the third day of the conference, Diana Grinin telephoned Blanka from an unregistered Swiss cell phone that she had bought for cash an hour before. Her husband, Major Grigori Grinin – architect of a new generation of targeted germ warfare – wished to defect. Diana had not wanted to meet face to face. Over the next two days, they had several phone discussions in which Diana relayed the terms for Grinin's defection to London.

Complex passwords and long recognition code words (often question-answer-confirmations) are ubiquitous in Intelligence. During the winter nights of early 2011, Grinin drilled Diana on their approach to Blanka and MI6, so they would not fall into any sort of KGB trap. Diana was the distant descendent of the Jewish writer Boris Pasternak who had converted to Russian Orthodoxy. Hiding and escape from persecution ran in her blood.

What Blanka remembered most from all the phone conversations occurred at the end of the first phone call, when Grinin's young wife tried to explain why her husband was defecting. 'He has had a change of heart,' she said.

Such was the importance that MI6 placed on Grinin's defection that the Russia Desk deployed thirty field agents on counter-surveillance at Heathrow, Helsinki and Zürich airports. Operation Zoo Time was led by assistant Russia Desk director, Jude Robinson, the younger of a pair of Australian brothers who were both agents Blanka had nicknamed after English novels she liked. The older Robinson, 'Crusoe,' had joined OhZone at the same time as Blanka. Later she christened the younger brother after Thomas Hardy's 1894 novel, *Jude the Obscure*, because 'Jude' Robinson seemed older than his thirty years, with the burdens of his love-life exceeding his ability to triumph.

Jude and Nearby had ridden shotgun as far as central Zürich. At that point Jude staked out the Swiss RailAway station while Nearby visited James Joyce's grave at Fluntern. Blanka got a taxi via the FIFA headquarters in the wooded hills of Zürichberg; her band's version of *Roads to Moscow* played in her head as she gazed at the trees. Bathed in the summer sunshine, Blanka made her way through the tourists at Zoologischer Garten carrying a battered knapsack. Although she had flown into Switzerland as a thirty-five year old Helsinki businesswoman, she now appeared as the sixty-year-old South African round-the-world traveller, Britt Potgeiter, in spectacles and a gray wig.

On her highly detoured train journey from Zürich-Kloten airport through central Zürich to Zoo Zürich in the Fluntern Quarter of District 7, Blanka had stopped for refreshments or the rest room no less than eight times. She changed her clothes and wig twice and eventually changed a black Samsonite carry-on case for the knapsack.

Blanka tore herself away from the Asian elephants swimming underwater and walked towards the tigers. A rare pair of Sumatran tiger twins had just come on display at the zoo; it was there that Blanka met Diana for the first time. She was wearing a white rose in her hair, and looked quite beautiful, Blanka thought.
Blanka stood beside her and spoke quietly:
'*Was ist in einem Namen?*' [What is in a name? [6]]
Diana replied, in broken German, 'That which we call a rose by any other name would smell as sweet.'
Blanka looked into Diana's blue eyes and acknowledged, again in perfect German, 'So Romeo would, were he not Romeo called, retain that dear perfection which he owes.'
'Without that title,' Diana firmly responded.

They looked closely at the beautiful tiger cubs and smiled naturally. 'Everything is agreed' Blanka said under her breath.
'Is River Heights central?' whispered Diana.
'Almost next to Big Ben.' Blanka looked at Diana's tummy and

smiled. 'You're pregnant,' she said. 'And with twin girls'.

'Jesus!' Diana said, astonished. 'You OhZones don't miss a trick.'

Blanka tapped her eyes and said, 'Enhanced vision comes in handy. When are they due?'

'March,' answered Diana. She took the white rose from her hair, held it so they could both smell it (the aroma of angels, remembered Diana, rarefied and pure) and handed it to Blanka. Then she walked away, having discretely picked up the battered knapsack.

Blanka lingered with the Sumatran tigers, admiring their strength and dignity even in captivity. Meanwhile Diana was soon gazing out the window of the westwards RailAway train at the nondescript suburbs of District 7. She went on to retrieve two empty attaché cases from a luggage locker at the SBB terminal, District 1. One hour, one bus and one discarded knapsack later, Diana crossed west over the River Limmat again, this time by tram, and got off with the attaché cases at Bahnhofstrasse, District 1, the most expensive street for retail property in Europe. She turned into number 9, the main office of the quiet canton bank, Zürcher Kantonalbank.

In a plush basement office she was served a Rosabaya coffee. The attaché cases beside her contained the British Government's hundred million US dollars that Blanka had brought as sweetener for Grinin to bring his Metapox expertise to the West. Diana furnished the bank official with Major Grinin's safe deposit box number and showed him the bronze key.

*A*t his first appearance on the *Steve Wright In The Afternoon* radio show, Major Grinin summed up their defection by saying: 'We decided to defect to the *West End*. We came to London Christmas shopping and never went home.'

On Thursday, 15th March 2012, on the seventh floor of St Thomas' Hospital, S.E.1 [half a mile along the South Bank from MI6] on nightingale Ward, Diana gave birth to healthy identical twins.

She had opted to labour in water and because her father (the renowned Moscow professor of obstetrics) was to attend in addition to the usual St. Thomas' team, the maternity unit had agreed to its first birth of a twin in water.

Later Diana proudly listened to Grinin quote her on Radio 2. 'Water, my beautiful wife has explained to me, encourages you to relax and can make your contractions seem less painful.' She loved her husband with typical Russian passion.

'Baby A', *Emma*, was the long water birth and weighed 5 lbs 4 oz. 'Baby B', *Olga*, was delivered thirty minutes later by Caesarean section and weighed 4 lbs 6 oz.

Grinin told the Radio 2 audience how pleased he was that his daughters were born at the hospital where Florence Nightingale (the hero of the Crimea, the last war between Britain and Russia) founded the first school of nursing.
Blanka, who was with Diana in the hospital, had whispered to her, 'She's one of my heroes though I'll be the first to admit that statistics go in one ear and come out the other. But I have her book *Cassandra*.'

On the day they were born, Emma and Olga became citizens of the E.U., the United Kingdom and the Borough of Lambeth. Four days later, when Blanka drove them and Diana home to River Heights, they became residents of Westminster. Not wanting to bother Diana with his often obscure preoccupations, Grinin kept his observation that Emma and Olga were born on the Ides of March to himself ℧

The Jericho Café

*A cheerful little station, very much like any
other provincial railway stop: a small square
framed by tall chestnuts and paved with yellow
gravel. And now the guards are being posted
along the rails, across the beams, in the
green shade of the Silesian chestnuts, to
form a tight circle around the ramp* [7]

1945, TADEUSZ BOROWSKI –
THIS WAY FOR THE GAS, LADIES AND GENTLEMEN

Three Years Later: Tuesday, March 10, 2015
Lamb's Conduit Street, London W.C.1, UK

*M*I6's treatment of Grinin since his defection had been far
from what Blanka and Diana had hoped for. Blanka was horri-
fied at C's attempts to force the Nobel Laureate microbiologist to
manufacture Metapox for Britain. She had hoped to minimize
C's interference, but she soon learned how far C was willing to
go. A street robbery C had arranged as a warning had been clum-
sily done and C's contractors had not counted on the old Russian's strength and agility. Grinin refused to be robbed quietly
and had knocked one of the men unconscious. In the confusion,

another fired, hitting Grinin in the right arm. The bullet had done so much damage that what was left of Grinin's arm below the elbow had to be amputated. Though the British public believed the story about the Russian KGB being responsible, no one in Intelligence was fooled. When an MI6 director provoked C about the robbery, C retorted, 'He came to London all smiles, thinking it'd be an easy number. I bet he's not grinin' now.'

To keep in contact with Grinin, Blanka had adopted the Jericho Café in Bloomsbury as an off-the-grid rendezvous. The Jericho was far from MI6 headquarters across the river but only a hundred yards from Holborn Police Station. She had friends in the Met and regarded police as less dishonest than spies. The Grade II listed pub, The Lamb, favoured by writers Charles Dickens, Sylvia Plath and Ted Hughes was at the top of the road. Less than half a mile from Hitler's chosen London headquarters, the Jericho was also on Grinin's regular route from his penthouse at River Heights on Victoria Embankment S.W.1, to the British Library N.W.1, where he spent much of his free time.

While his arm was healing Grinin had a lot of time to think, and so did Blanka. Too many things were going wrong: Felicity's promotion to U7, Grinin's mutilation, Oxberry's diagnosis of her kidney disease and being tied to a dialysis machine. And the dreams, the visions – Blanka wasn't sure what to call them – that seemed to be pressing against her since she started the dialysis. They hit her when she was at her most vulnerable.

★

*I*t's the wrong notepaper, Blanka mumbled to herself, her eyes shut. 'Blanka?' a heavily accented Russian voice interrupted. A man's voice. It was slightly crazy sounding as if from a genius or a maniac. 'Blanka?' It should be the *OhZone* notepaper with the lovely '℧' symbol at the top of it. The notepaper mattered, Blanka told herself, ever since 'The Cadre' had been phased out fifteen years ago and replaced by her ethical hit unit. We get the target with no collateral damage, we keep a clean slate. She was proud of that. So the notepaper mattered. Or did it? Was killing ever ethical? Agent ℧1 hadn't turned out so ethical. Moonlighting on a celebrity assassination, and then deserting. Now he was on both OhZone and CIA wanted lists. Our private hit list. The killing never stops. Your own mother…

'Blanka!' the Russian was getting irritated. 'It's your move.' Blanka's eyes had been half-closed. Abruptly she opened them and focused on a pawn, red as blood. She had been gripping it so tightly her fingers had turned pale. As she turned it over and over, the thought went through her head: my blood. The orchestral music of Samuel Barber played from the café stereo; she had always liked the music at the Jericho. When had she picked the pawn up?

'Blanka, Blanka. Miles away as usual. You've been dreaming.' She recognized the voice now. The man sitting across from her was an elderly, thickly bearded, bear-of-a-man, Major Grigori Grinin. She winced when her eyes fell on his stump.
'Sorry, Grigori, I'm easily distracted. But that's all. I don't dream.'
'I knew Kitty when you were in a gym-slip. Of course you dream.'
'I was never in a fucking gym-slip,' snapped Blanka. 'I was twenty.'
'Which ear was your mother deaf in?'
'The left, don't start that again.'
At the table behind them a gay couple were drinking white wine. One whispered to the other, 'That's Grigori Grinin the Russian defector, I heard him on the radio yesterday.'

On the table between Blanka and Grinin was a chessboard. For a few seconds the ceiling light flickered upon it, then the music died and the room settled into semi-darkness. 'Now the lights go out,'

Grinin exclaimed. 'How can anyone concentrate? Not that anyone needs to concentrate when they play you.'

'Enough already,' exclaimed Blanka draining her wine glass, 'Jesus Joseph and Mary.'

Grinin refilled Blanka's glass from a bottle of Burgundy and handed it to her. 'Of course, we Librans don't usually swear. *Na zdorovie,*' he said chinking glasses. 'To Librans.'

'Na zdorovie, to Librans,' replied Blanka. She put the pawn down and frowned at her white pieces. Her OhZone super-sensitive hearing was picking up a humming sound. She looked around. It sounded like *bees.* She looked out the window at the snow as it fell on the street, glowing eerily in the afternoon gloom. Blanka kept bees, but it couldn't be bees, she thought, it's far too cold. Some of the snowflakes seemed unusual though: moving erratically almost like tiny sparks. Then she clocked the shops and restaurants, the Great Ormond Street Hospital for Children. They were all dark. Apparently the electricity was out for at least a block.

'This never happens,' she said.

'Britain feels like a third world country,' Grinin grumbled. 'Your National Rail system is a disgrace. A forty year backlog of essential engineering work. And what do they do? As a KGB man, I can tell you! They *hide it.*'

'From the public?'

'From the public, from each other, from God! Who knows? Now, *what* about my soufflé?'

The gay couple toyed with their iPhones in vain, 'There's no signal,' said the first. 'There's no *battery,*' said the second.

Blanka signalled an employee who was peering out of the kitchen door. 'This gentleman wants to know about his soufflé,' she told him. The middle-aged sous chef seemed particularly flustered by the power outage. 'My soufflé, young man!' Grinin growled, squinting at him. 'I am here in the dark playing chess with my nitwit friend and the only thing that will save this afternoon is a good soufflé!' As the sous chef scrambled to the kitchen Blanka leaned over and whispered, 'You don't have to frighten him.' Grinin assumed an outraged and dignified pose, 'When one *looks like Rasputin*, one must sometimes *act like Rasputin.*'

'Yes,' said Blanka. 'But my Rasputin dances the tables.'

'You tricked me,' Grinin said smiling.

'No, Steve Wright was the one who made you a celebrity here. I only encouraged you to dance.'

It had been Blanka's brainchild to introduce Grinin and Diana to two of her most interesting friends at the exclusive nightclub *Wilion* (where she DJ'd) around the corner from Berkley Square, W.1. One friend was the African-American OhZone chief scientist, Dr Ray Oxberry, and the other was the MI6 chief psychiatrist Dr Don Fox. Both were in their seventies, as was Grinin. Steve Wright, a London radio personality, had arrived just as Blanka asked the night's DJ to play the 1978 hit *Rasputin* by the black German group Boney M. It went, 'There lived a certain man in Russia long ago / He was big and strong, in his eyes a flaming glow / Most people looked at him with terror and with fear / But to Moscow chicks he was such a lovely dear.' Using his cell phone, Steve Wright filmed the whole thing. The sight of the three bearded academics serenading the heavily pregnant Diana with stylized Russian dancing, had been an instant hit on YouTube.

Grinin started appearing on Monday in a spot called *Grigori Spins* on Steve's BBC radio show – and *Rasputin* became his theme song. Over several weeks, he spoke about his love of chess and helping his wife with her efforts for animal conservation, and played a favourite hit. He also talked about the robbery, praising the NHS (Britain's public health service) and playing down his heroics and the trauma of his arm. 'My wife likes to play nurse,' he declared. 'Although she, like me, is a doctor of biology. So we play doctors also, and doctor and nurse...'

Because C was officially responsible for Grinin, he had been summoned by Prime Minister, Jermaine Corduroy. With the general election only eight weeks away, Mr Corduroy was grasping at straws to boost his flagging popularity. To C's intense displeasure, the P.M. commended Grinin's radio appearances, saying he wanted to bring the NHS, politics and the Arts closer together. As C followed the Foreign Secretary, L.B.J., out of 10 Downing Street that day, two words buzzed in C's head: *Piss* and *artists*.

'How strange it was,' Grinin told Blanka, recalling club *Wilion*. 'Boney M, of all people, had three hits in the UK Top Twenty when you were born in 1978. *Rasputin*, as well as *Rivers of Babylon* and *Brown Girl In The Ring*.'
'I did not know that,' said Blanka, not even pretending to be interested.
As she struggled to make her move, Grinin pondered the mysteries of synchronicity.
Blanka's mother, Kitty – who he had saved from death in St. Petersburg – was then murdered in Rome on Thursday December 30th. On the anniversary of the 1916 assassination, by MI6 agents, of Grigori Rasputin in St. Petersburg. Boney M's front man, Bobby Farrell, had died of a heart attack ten years after Kitty's murder, also on Thursday December 30th. Also in St Petersburg

> *Ra – Ra – Rasputin lover of the Russian Queen*
> *They didn't quit, they wanted his head*
> *Ra – Ra – Rasputin Russia's greatest love machine*
> *And so they shot him 'til he was dead*

Two murders, three unexpected deaths. What were the odds of these synchronicities happening at random in the universe?

Three hundred and sixty five in eight hundred thousand million. Approximately. And Valentina wants me back in Petersburg? He studied Blanka. Thursdays for dying, he mused. The sous chef approached their table. 'Where's my soufflé?' Grinin demanded. 'It was ruined,' replied the sous chef (with an Australian accent) 'When the power went.'

Blanka wondered if Grinin knew the sous chef was part of her undercover team: Crusoe agent Ʊ7 (the elder Robinson brother). He probably did.
'You cook on gas,' Grinin roared. 'You don't need electricity. Make me another!' Deeply unhappy with his cover, Crusoe frowned and retreated into the kitchen. 'It's your move,' Grinin repeated to Blanka, waving the stump of his right arm at the chessboard. 'You're clearly not on form. I will checkmate you in two moves.'

As Blanka returned to the chessboard, she made eye contact with a freckled young woman sitting at a table near the front window. An academic type, with spectacles and hippy-chic clothes, she was sipping on a drink and had a copy of James Joyce's *Ulysses* open in front of her. Blanka looked back at Grinin, whose eyes were on his end game. I wonder if he knows about her too, Blanka thought. She smiled to herself: he's KGB, he'll know

*D*isguise played a big part in 'Intelligence' – a term used in place of 'spying,' which was outlawed, to make *what they did* seem clever, mind numbing and superior to what ordinary people did. It was language as verbal disguise.

To disguise themselves in the physical world, spies were dressed in appropriate attire. So the woman in the window, Nearby, now closely resembled the star of *Charmed,* Rose McGowan, but with freckles and glasses to boot.

After fifty hours coaching by 'Arms', MI6's chief firearms officer – and two years carrying a pistol when on Ops for Blanka – Nearby had gotten used to the extra twenty five ounces weight in her Iceni handbag. The Sig Sauer P320 Rx Compact polymer semi-automatic was chambered for the smallest rounds. She didn't carry a spare clip and had never had to aim it outside the firing range. Arms had modified it with a Dak (Double Action Kellerman). If she ever had to fire it in anger, the Dak ensured she couldn't jam the mechanism by not squeezing the trigger hard enough.

Unusually, Nearby had done her nails which were adorned by pale green polish with gold bits on. She was practicing for a birthday party the coming Sunday when her nails would be silver and gold – and she would wear a ball gown! Nearby imagined Arms taking her there. In her fantasies, Arms and her Russia Desk bosses, Russia and Jude, appropriately dressed as the Three Musketeers, swirled around her defending her honour from sinister assailants as she ascended white marble steps, to an elegant ballroom.

Fortunately for Major Grinin's security, Nearby was only one of five agents carrying out Grinin's CCSP (covert counter-surveillance and protection). The fourth, Adele Wasson of the CIA, was parked down the street in a Grensons delivery van. In the back was one of OhZone's technical officers, a young man nicknamed 'Farringdon' (the part of London where he lived) surrounded by blacked-out monitors and counter-surveillance equipment. He was however speaking to agent Ʊ5 Sokol Comarova, over his gray-screen portable ƱScanner, which was working fine.

At various times, The Jericho Café had been frequented by Helena

Blavatsky, W.B. Yeats, Oscar Wilde and James Joyce. In addition to the cheap paperback of Joyce's *Ulysses,* Nearby's table was graced by a Virgin Mary. She was only pretending to read the novel.

Surely everyone must have to pretend to read it, thought Nearby. But Nearby pretended to read *Ulysses* not because of its difficulty (it *was* difficult to read but she had a degree from Trinity College, had read it several times, studied it in fact) but because she carried it with her on Ops to relieve the boredom. It was foolish to read on the job, especially when her job was to observe the world around for signs of hidden threats, but with *Ulysses* she could simply dip into a phrase or two and immediately connect to the richness of Joyce's Dublin, and her home.

Nearby put her hands behind her head and stretched. Her gaze took in the street. In the cab of the Grenson's delivery van, Adele sat impassively. Inside Nearby's bag, a message from Adele displayed on her ℧Scanner: 20/20 clear in all directions. Nearby closed the bag and returned to the paperback. Being near the window, she could still see the page she had randomly turned to. Page 32. The character on the page, Mr Deasy, had been pinching the wings of his nose and slagging off Jews and women

> A woman brought sin into the world. For a woman who was no better than she should be, Helen, the runaway wife of Menelaus, ten years the Greeks made war on Troy.

Nearby checked on Grinin and Blanka's game. Grinin was capturing Blanka's white bishop with his characteristic Russian zest

> A faithless wife first brought the strangers to our shore here

Misogynist and anti-Semite, thought Nearby. Done my research: Diana's part Jewish. Emma and Olga are so sweet, can't wait to see their faces on Sunday. They won't be without a father if I can help it.

She closed the book, sipped her Virgin Mary and her thoughts returned to Felicity, and Jude her poor husband.

A faithless wife: that suits Felicity Robinson to a tee. But I failed to get into OhZone and she succeeded. Forty days in the OhZone Machine. What a long time it takes to transform one of God's creatures. Is Felicity God's creature? Are humans God's creatures? Or are we some infection of the Earth, like Metapox. But some of us are Cain's descendants. A slug goes into a pupa to come out a butterfly, a beautiful thing. Are Cain's descendants beautiful too? Is there a beauty, a saving grace in them?

As she looked at pretty Blanka and handsome old Grinin, she thought about her own life before meeting Blanka. In Dublin and London women like Felicity had always had the social poise, the quick one-liners to put her down so readily. Felicity's a slug, I bet there aren't days and nights enough to turn her into a butterfly. But Blanka had made her feel good about herself, had encouraged her to sing in the choir and now she intoned the *Credo*. Her stutter had lessened too. Nearby turned, made eye contact with Adele in the van and viewed the Scanner inside her bag again: clear in all directions.

She eyed Grinin intently. And here is *Mr Biology*; or should I say: here is *Mr Death*? – the creator of a terrible new terror: a targeted bio-weapon – just a few tables away. Metapox. It was *the* topic in Wonderland at the moment. From Genghis Khan to Rasputin, thought Nearby. But Grinin's a lovely old fella, how could he do such a thing? She watched Blanka pondering where to move the white queen. Trying so desperately to make a difference. Nearby glanced up when she heard Grinin speak in his gruff Rasputin voice.
'My soufflé ruined, power cuts in 21st century London, whoever heard of such a thing. And in Bloomsbury!'
'First world problems,' suggested Blanka unhelpfully. 'Compared to what many others face.'

As she spoke the lights and heating came back on. In seconds the shops and the Children's Hospital came back to life followed by the honking of car horns as the traffic lights shone red and green once more. In the distance, alarms began to howl.

'You see,' she said, 'Normal service will be resumed shortly.'

Nearby felt her gold-colored iPhone vibrate back to life in her jeans pocket.

Nearby liked being one of Blanka's Girls, and she had great respect for the KGB-trained Sokol, Blanka's second-in-command. If Sokol had been running the unit she would have drowned Felicity in the River Thames rather than let her become an OhZone. Nearby tried to make light of her failure to beat Felicity. But she was hit by the irony that for forty days and forty nights, the gay Dr Oxberry, who no one had ever had a bad word to say for, had laboured uncomplainingly to transform a self-confessed racist anti-Semite homophobe, who despised everything Blanka stood for, into a super-woman.

Grigori Grinin looked around for his soufflé – in vain. 'But where is my dinner!' Nearby smiled, returned to counter-surveillance and pretending to read *Ulysses*.

Blanka's Fairphone cell came back to life too – in her Mini Cooper near Wembley Park tube station where they'd left it. According to the grid, Blanka was probably with a boyfriend who worked at Dollis Hill Ecology Centre and trained with Kilburn Cosmos R.F.C. Blanka captained the Ladies team, *Kilburn Cosmonauts*, and they had beat Harlequins Ladies 34 – 29 in their last game.

Sokol was on her way there now. After Blanka's rugby training tonight, Sokol would drive her to Poole Harbour in Dorset, close to Castle Monkton where an MI6 conference on Metapox was scheduled for the next day

2.3

South of the river, in the firing range deep under MI6 Head-quarters, Felicity Robinson was trying out her newly acquired pair of P321 Full Size pistols. She'd graduated as Ʊ7 against the wishes of Oxberry, Fox, Hart, Russia, Blanka, Sokol, the CIA – just the day before. Now she dived athletically across the floor aiming a 321 at a spot on the padded concrete wall. Then she rolled across the floor aiming it in one direction then another and revealing the large tattoo on her left arm: a fearsome portrait of Genghis Khan with a black swastika hidden within it.

'Go,' she yelled. The lights dimmed and moving targets of human shapes appeared in different doorways and windows in rapid succession, two or three at a time. Felicity emptied the clip of ten .45 FCP rounds – tearing gaping holes in the heads of the first ten targets: six men, two women and two children.

The lights came back on and Felicity jumped up looking disappointed. Arms, a middle-age man with an uneasy face, approached. 'You're not supposed,' he said, 'to shoot the children. Your previous –'
She stepped closer to Arms allowing him a good view of her breasts. Arms lost his train of thought. He hadn't had sex in a while and he wasn't going to argue with a débutante OhZone with a loaded Sig down her pants. He held out his hand for the first 321. She handed it over and he confirmed that it was empty.
'The other one?' he said and looked at her expectantly. Felicity smiled and produced the loaded pistol from her jeans. 'OhZones use Sigs chambered for 9mm Luger or point 357. Why d'you want to use point forty-five FCP?' he asked.
Felicity put on her seductive face, 'I intend to make an impact.'

'You need to look,' she added, bending over further and reaching into her Bulgari handbag. She removed a memo and handed it to him. The MI6 notepaper was signed 'C' in green ink

Re. Testing of point 45 depleted uranium rounds

Chief Firearms Officer Evans,
Newly appointed agent ℧7 is hereby authorised to use the above for test purposes, with immediate effect.

He nodded, 'Don't you have a home to go to?'
'I'm running Cloud Nine tonight,' Felicity ran her tongue over her lips. 'Come along to the bar.'
'I don't have time for the Wonder bar. How come you're running it? You only got back from Paris yesterday.'
'I'm popular.'
'Yeah, you're trouble. Has anybody ever told you that?'
'Trouble looking for a good time. Isn't that what every man wants? A little trouble, just to spice things up?' She pulled the 321 out of his hand. 'And you're single. Where's the harm? I was hoping you would give me private lessons.'
'You'd need extra-thick sandbags to use depleted uranium rounds.'
'I know you've got extra-thick. I've been watching you.'
Arms could feel his resolve crumbling. 'Man's gotta be a fool,' he said. 'You not a little trouble, you're a whole lot of trouble.'
Felicity smiled. 'You can handle it, just like the uranium rounds. Wouldn't you like to handle it? I'm running Cloud Nine again Sunday night. We can chat and then come in here.'
Arms took a deep breath, 'All right, Furness,' he said calling her by her maiden name. Although she had been married two months she didn't bother to correct him   ℧

Two Birds With One Stone

*I have been asked whether in the years to come it will
be possible to kill forty million American people
in a single night. The answer is yes.*

*1945, JULIUS ROBERT OPPENHEIMER
- FATHER OF THE ATOMIC BOMB*

Wednesday, March 11, 2015
Castle Monkton, Dorsetshire

*A*midst the last heavy snowfall of that winter, Blanka
mounted her favourite stallion Caesar, a seven-year-old white
Lusitano her brother Will had given her on her thirty-fifth
birthday. Waving goodbye to Sokol, she turned her back on Poole
Harbour and rode off towards Castle Monkton. Underneath her
quilted Barbour, Blanka wore a T-shirt adorned with the 'PADI'
logo and the words 'Dive Master Instructor'. At her collarbone
hung a different badge, a kidney dialysis cannula leading to a
Dacron cuff. A bronze Celtic short-sword swinging at her side
was a humorous birthday gift. Not only had she been tagged
Queen Boudica, but OhZone Division were referred to as the *Iceni*.
Professor Hart had given her the ancient weapon in September
having exhumed it from the murky UK seabed North of Cromer.

MI6 ran Castle Monkton as a training facility for Intelligence officers and special forces. It still bore the scars of a brief but brutal siege during the English Civil War, the missing pieces of battlement testament to the effectiveness of ancient cannonballs.

Caesar's hoofs clattered over the castle's wooden drawbridge as two Royal Marines sentries raised the barrier and saluted. Blanka waved and wiped some strange flat snowflakes from her eyes as Caesar trotted into the courtyard, where a six-foot-eight tall figure waited for Blanka. The captured Russian spy, Andrei Petrov, acting as Blanka's groom, had resisted MI6's year-long grilling of him before he was handed over to OhZone. Blanka slipped her boots from the stirrups, reined her horse to a halt and vaulted from the saddle. Landing skilfully in the snow Blanka handed Petrov her riding crop and had begun walking towards the castle keep when her left knee suddenly buckled. She quickly regained her balance, looked over at Petrov and said, 'You didn't see that.'
The Russian bowed his head slightly and fed back to Blanka the words she had impressed upon him during his interrogation, 'Warrior, know thyself.'

A few seconds later, a Royal Marines sergeant escorted Blanka into the vaulted stone hall that served as the conference room and closed the door behind her. C (unimposing man, medium height and build) sat, surrounded by directors, signing orders in green ink *with his right hand*. He did not look up. C's personal assistant, Miss Banks who poured Blanka tea, was known only as Miss Banks, but the eight directors had titles in line with MI6's names policy. The oldest, a petite silver haired woman, 'Devices', ruled the realm of technical innovations, gadgets and the quartermaster's stores. She looked up from the agenda and smiled, as Miss Banks handed Blanka a white and blue *40 Commando* cup and saucer, with a friendly, 'Good going, Blanka?'
'Hard underfoot,' said Blanka as she hopped onto the boardroom

table next to Devices. Once seated, she took out a bag of Lindors, offered it to Devices and Miss Banks and took a couple herself. As Blanka swung her booted legs back and forth, Devices and the director on the other side, Bio, examined the turquoise inlays on the hilt of the Celtic short-sword. Bio reached past Blanka and magically produced a Lindor from behind Blanka's ear. 'If you keep eating chocolates, you'll turn into one.'
'Hmm, will you eat me?' Blanka smiled.
'What, again?' Bio winked, popping the chocolate into her mouth. C glared across the table at the pair, as Blanka leaned over and whispered, 'Well, there's no such thing as a free lunch.'
Bio and Blanka saw more of each other since Bio had succeeded to director a year before, upon the death of her superior in an accident with drug-resistant plague bacteria.

As the wait continued, the words of an E minor guitar strum Blanka's grandfather had taught her, went through Blanka's head. America's *A Horse With No Name* always made her smile on the inside as she thought of spies and disguises and the ocean. Blanka thought of Dewey Bunnell's explanation that *Horse* was 'a metaphor for a vehicle to get away from life's confusion into a quiet, peaceful place.'

The laughter of two men echoing in the castle corridor outside the room made it apparent to everyone that Jude Robinson was briefing his superior, Russia. They all knew Russia's laugh, and his sense of humour. The simple bass tab going through Blanka's head was interrupted by Miss Banks, an octave higher, 'Blanka!'
Blanka looked at her, then past her to Russia as he walked into the conference room.
'Oh my God,' Blanka said, and burst out laughing.
Russia nodded to the four women and approached her. 'I wanted to check you were paying attention.'
Blanka nodded. She was the only person present replete with OhZone vision – in the UV to X-ray bandwidth – enabling her to

do useful things like seeing inside her handbag from the outside. It also meant she could see through doors, people's clothes, and so on. 'You got my attention alright,' said Blanka. 'An English *cricket box* if I'm not mistaken?'

'Yes, lead lined,' smiled Russia, as Miss Banks passed him a cup of tea. 'Fully polonium-proof. Devices knocked it up for me.'

The male Director of Interrogation, 'Probe', who was chairing this meeting, approached patting his pockets. He was the eldest director after Devices and appeared to share with her a certain mellowness that age brought to some. In fact, unbeknown to him, he was experiencing the severe symptoms of Stage 3 Lyme Disease. 'The way things are going, you don't know when you're going to need one,' he said joining in the joke. Seeing Blanka's short-sword, he brandished his old-time MI6-issue sword-stick with a flourish, making them laugh. Then he turned to Devices, 'I seem to have left my reading glasses at H.Q. Wonderland.' Handing Probe her pair of half-eye reading glasses, Devices said, 'You need looking after.'

Blanka thought about Grinin's distance glasses. He hadn't been wearing them yesterday. She was worried he'd walk under a number 15 bus. Diana nagged him into wearing them, but he was vain and the rest of the time he didn't bother. Probe wandered to the front of the room, waved his copy of the agenda and cleared his throat. The meeting had officially begun.

At the front was a wall-mounted blackboard labelled 'Top Secret: Metapox Weapon for Britain.' While the Intelligence services of all nations had embraced state-of-the-art Comms, Probe and C still recognized the value of media that could be erased completely without leaving a trace (chalk), or swallowed whole (rice paper). As Miss Banks dimmed the lights, a bead-like microbe, the Metapox host cell, shimmered on a projection screen. It was labelled in Russian, with the English translation

Spirochaeta grininensis

Probe looked over the half-eye glasses at those around the table, pausing to catch the eye of each in turn. Slowly they stopped talking.

'Metapox, gentlemen,' Probe said in his best official voice.
'And ladies,' added Bio, raising her eyes at Devices.
'And Queen Boudica,' Probe added with a chuckle, 'from OhZone.'
C mouthed, 'Get on with it,' at Probe. Bio cued the projector and another electron micrograph slide came up beside the first – showing the host cells filled with four different species of virus, labelled in Russian and translated by her. 'Metapox, the ultimate germ-warfare agent,' he announced. 'Explain the name please, Bio.'

Bio looked up, smiled at Probe and reeled off the science. 'The Soviet Union came into possession of Japanese World War Two cell-wall-deficient, virulent, spirochete bacteria.' Probe used his sword-stick as a pointer to tap the bead-like spirochete on the screen. 'The brilliant team of Grigori Grinin and Clyde Carlos,' continued Bio, 'genetically modified the bacteria DNA to code for lethal viruses, and made the virus-size-spirochete-beads airborne.'

'Thank you, Bio. One virus is none other than our old friend, smallpox,' Probe said excitedly, tapping the smallpox DNA with the sword-stick. Bio nodded. 'As Bio has explained to us before and most of you should know, just two dozen contaminated perfume bottles will spread Metapox in a few months: through a whole population. Then the four virus strains lie dormant – until activated by the high-frequency signal – when they rupture and kill the population in...'
'Forty eight to ninety six hours,' confirmed Bio.
'This Weapon-of-Mass-Destruction, what's its fatality rate?' asked 'Asia' (Sam Patel, the British Indian director of the Asia Desk).
'Ninety-nine point five to one hundred percent,' answered Bio.

'In short,' Probe flatly declared, 'the population of a whole nation can be infected and then held to ransom, under threat of death.' Total silence followed his words.

'To counter this threat, we have in our custody the Nobel Laureate inventor of Metapox, Major Grigori Grinin.'
'He's not in our custody. He's our guest,' interjected Asia.
'Oh, yes. So he is,' admitted Probe, laughing. 'I forgot.'
'He's in our hands. That's the main thing,' growled C to Miss Banks, as she poured him more tea and added his sweetener pills.
'Yes, well, we want him to manufacture the Metapox for Britain – '
'And our NATO allies,' interrupted Asia.
'Of course,' Probe acknowledged, glancing sideways at C, his expression and voice unchanged. 'Our intent is to manufacture it as a deterrent to those who might use it against us.' He paused again.

'The reason for Major Grinin's defection is no secret to anyone in Intelligence. With the collusion of someone high in the Russian KGB, four Metapox weapons were sold into the hands of the Kazak Mafia. It obviously adds urgency to the situation. Our intent has been to persuade the Major to reproduce the weapon here. To this end we spent a billion pounds on the most sophisticated microbiology laboratory in the world.'

'*Biology Farm*,' said Devices.
'It's name is Facility Q,' Bio said coldly.
'Why is it underground in the Channel Islands?' asked Asia, studying a manila square cut folder (color: red) labelled

FACILITY Q (ISLAND OF JERSEY) – TOP SECRET
Release is Liable to Cause Considerable Loss of Life or International Diplomatic Incidents

'Not - relevant,' barked C. 'Move on, Chairman.'
'I mean, what's Jersey ever done to anyone?' persisted Asia. 'You're

making the deadliest weapon in human history underneath it.'
Probe looked sheepishly at Asia, 'So far Major Grinin has not
started work. As a result, we are left with three options.'
He spun a whiteboard and, in his droning professorial voice, sum-
marized the three options. The first, titled 'The Five Techniques,'
he identified as the methods developed on IRA detainees in North-
ern Ireland. The second option, 'C's Method,' he described as
similar to the first, 'but with a lot more blood.' Comments and sar-
donic laughter ran around the table. C glared at Probe.

'These are harsh times,' he announced to everyone, 'and require
harsh actions. My methods are born out of necessity. We are all
Crown Servants. As a loyal servant of the Queen, I don't hesitate to
get my hands a little dirty when the situation calls for it.'

C's supporters nodded their assent; those opposed to him looked
away in embarrassment. Blanka could see the anger behind Russia's
calm face, the impenetrable mask of a seasoned diplomat.
Addressing the third option on the whiteboard: 'Blanka's Method.'
Probe continued, 'We turn now to our third and final option.
Though I cordially disagree with OhZone 4 on many subjects, her
soft interrogation techniques do yield remarkable results.'
'Remarkable and fast,' put in Devices.
'Colleagues,' Blanka called out as she stood back from the table.
'Although I'm grateful for your recognition of OhZone's
successes, I will not participate in a plan that increases the
amount of Metapox in the world.'
A buzz went around the room.

C dramatically rose from his position at the table. 'Queen Boudica,'
he asked with exaggerated dignity, 'Do I take it you won't interro-
gate Grinin?'
Blanka turned to Devices, Bio and Miss Banks and mouthed the
words 'Excuse me,' then turned back to C.

'Fuck you,' she said softly, smiling. 'Germ warfare is banned by all civilized countries. Everyone here knows that.'

'It's for *protection*,' Probe added, attempting to defuse the situation. 'We wouldn't *use* the Metapox. Your methods are formidable,' he pleaded. 'You had Petrov eating out of your hand after a few days at your torture farm –'

'It's referred to as *animal* farm,' Devices interrupted.

'Animal *sanctuary*,' Blanka corrected with a slight bite of her lip. Devices acknowledged the correction with a nod. 'On one of your lovely islands, I so enjoyed visiting –'

'Gentlemen,' shouted Probe trying to restore order.

'And ladies,' said Devices. 'I've been putting up with this for fifteen years.'

'He's hopeless,' Bio whispered to Devices, before calmly raising her arm and turning to Blanka. '*Colleague*,' Bio said smiling. 'Please clarify your statement for us. You can't or you *won't* get Grinin to make Metapox for us?'

'I won't.' Blanka put her short-sword on the table and placed her hand firmly on top of it. 'If I could get into Facility N and Porton Down, I'd eliminate Britain's entire stock of germ warfare weapons.'

Bio and most other directors muttered their disagreement. Seeing his opportunity, C pulled a laminated portrait photograph from a manila square cut folder (color: buff) and strode with it towards the front of the room. Holding aloft the photograph, he pronounced 'Gentlemen, let me announce a fourth option.' Turning to Probe he added, 'It's in the addendum to the agenda.' Probe turned to the additional page, which no one else had.

'Our first fast-track candidate Felicity Robinson,' continued C, 'Has just graduated from the OhZone program. She is primed and ready to bring her skills to bear on Major Grinin.'

Blanka could barely contain her anger. Almost of its own accord, the short-sword in her hand flew the length of the table and pinned the photograph of Felicity to the blackboard behind C.

Miss Banks screamed. Devices, enjoying the fun, exclaimed 'Good shot,' as Probe drew his sword from his sword-stick and waved it in the air.

Bio laughed, reduced to tears, and C was too shocked to speak. Blanka did her deep breathing exercises and checked her notes. One by one, the nine directors grew quiet and looked at her.

'I also have a further option. There is another, less bloody way,' she told them.

'It is just this kind of irrational and unwarranted act,' C shouted, angrily pointing at the photo pinned by the sword to the blackboard, 'That brings home to us the importance of re-orienting OhZone. If that is not a bloody act, I don't know what is.'

'I don't see any blood,' Blanka replied slyly.

'You have not followed the required procedure!' C shot back. 'There is no fifth option on the agenda. Is there, Probe?

'Well...' stammered Probe, looking to Miss Banks who simply raised her eyebrows.

For the first time, Russia rose from his seat. He raised his hand dramatically, gestured to the short-sword, and in a deep, mock-Shakespearean voice intoned, 'Is this a dagger which I see before me?'

Miss Banks and most directors laughed, even Probe and Bio, breaking the tension. C sucked his teeth and made a point of not sitting down. 'Fellow directors,' Russia continued, returning to his normal voice. 'We can debate and vote to overrule required procedures, or we can just hear Miss Maguire out. I invited her here today. Major Grinin and the Metapox are surely in the province of the Russia Desk. The leader of OhZone has in my opinion a new and power-

ful alternative and I ask you to consider what she says.'
Having finished, he ushered Blanka forward and sat down. C
glared at her and reluctantly returned to his seat.

'Article I of the Biological Weapons Convention,' began Blanka,
'Sponsored in 1972 by Britain, bans all germ warfare weapons.'
'Get real,' heckled C, 'the Russians and Kazaks have it, and we
don't.'
'Grigori Grinin is a haunted man,' Blanka continued. 'He's haunted
by the shadow of his creation. The shadow of a genetically modi-
fied Frankenstein –'
'It's already cost him his right arm,' echoed Devices.
Now it was Probe's turn to glare. 'You of all people, Octavia,' he
snapped at Devices, before turning back to the room.
'He lost his arm *in a robbery*. I will not allow malicious rumours to
go unchallenged!'
Ignoring Probe, Asia added, 'Corduroy has gone on record to rule
out possession of biological weapons.'
C snorted, 'On this subject, at least, the P.M. says what we tell him to.'
'Metapox is a monster Major Grinin created,' Blanka persisted. 'A
monster he now wants desperately to destroy.'

C laughed out loud. 'Destroy! He's filibustering so the Russians
can *destroy us* when they please.' He stood up between the table
and Blanka and whispered to her, 'You've got two hopes. No hope
and Bob Hope.' A couple of the die-hards heard, and groaned at
C's old joke.
Devices solemnly shook her head and stood up, scraping her chair
on the stone floor. She faced C.
'C,' she said. He turned about.
'Stop your bullying.'
Russia turned to Miss Banks, who'd stopped writing, 'We need
this in the minutes, with a copy to Dr Fox. We've got *required
procedures* now to deal with bullying and intimidation.'

Probe pulled a sour face at C, and then gestured to Blanka to continue. 'Go on when you're ready, OhZone 4.'

'Thank you. My option is this. Major Grinin will make a *vaccine* against the Metapox.'
A hush came over the room and every set of eyes fell upon Blanka. 'A simple vaccine, and the world will be safe from this meta-weapon.'

C, lost for counter-argument, puffed out his cheeks, stuck his hands in his pockets and sat down again.
'Is it feasible?' queried Asia.
'I've discussed it with Major Grinin, and I quote,' Blanka answered pausing a moment to savour the look on C's face. 'A trans-genera vaccine can be devised to render all current and future Metapox generation weapons quite useless. And it can be made at Biology Farm.' She turned to the rest of the directors. 'That's the fifth option. You must decide if it's acceptable.'

Russia walked towards the blackboard, winking at Blanka as he passed. Reaching the board, he pulled the short-sword from the photo of Felicity and raised both objects into the air.
'Gentlemen, *and ladies,*' he said, 'We have *options.*'
He waved Blanka's sword. 'The Iceni approach – a vaccine.'
He raised Felicity's photograph over his head, 'Or C's fast-track OhZone recruit – Mrs Robinson.'
He handed Blanka back the sword. With a wink, he gave Bio Felicity's photo, to pass back to C. He then turned to Probe.
'Let's put it to a vote shall we, Chairman?'

As Blanka slipped her sword into its scabbard, she whispered, 'I trust I'm no longer needed.'
'You made your point,' he replied. 'The way your sword acts on its own, I'm glad I wore my cricket box.'

Blanka left the table and Miss Banks hurried to open the oak door. As she and Blanka stepped out into the castle corridor, Blanka reached for her cell phone and battery from a basket divided into sections. The other sections contained ten Lumia, LG, Samsung and Sony phones, and their batteries.

'Battery out until you reach your yard,' Miss Banks reminded her. 'And – well held.'

Blanka nodded, 'Thanks.'

The two women looked out through the medieval window at the floodlit courtyard, at the snow flakes falling on Andre Petrov as he rubbed down Caesar.

'He's a giant of a man,' commented Miss Banks, turning to look into Blanka's eyes.

'Yes, he is,' agreed Blanka.

Miss Banks gripped Blanka's hand in hers. 'Some men just think they're giants,' she said. 'And we have to be careful around them'

As Blanka reached her horse, Ma Baker's helicopter came into view out of the dark, descending with its landing lights flashing. Petrov held Caesar, calming him against the turbulence, as the Royal Marines sergeant marched towards them at the double. Saluting Blanka and indicating the helicopter, he shouted, 'OhZone 4, Ma'am, U.S. Embassy dispatch arriving for you. Will you come this way?'

In a secure room downstairs, with the Royal Marines sergeant on guard outside the door, the two passengers from the American helicopter – Adele Wasson and an older man in the uniform of a high ranking Naval officer – sat down with Blanka. Adele was a CIA Weapons of Mass Destruction expert; the officer carried a small metal case handcuffed to his left arm.

'This is Commander Gray, U.S. Navy,' Adele hurriedly explained as the officer shook hands with Blanka.
'He's currently deployed at our Embassy. He carries a Defcon 9 message from Langley.'

When Gray set the shiny aluminum case on the small table between them, Adele unlocked the handcuffs, punched a ten digit code into the case, and stepped aside to let Gray open the lid to reveal a state-of-the-art mobile Defcon Comms platform. When Gray powered it up using a key and another code, the Central Intelligence Agency emblem appeared together with a short message

> *CIA maximum security transmission — protocol Defcon 9 — for the eyes of Bronwyn Mary Brown only*

'Bronwyn Brown?' Gray looked uneasy.
'In The Company we're often given multiple identities,' Blanka said.
Adele went on to explain. 'Her grandfather was a four-star Admiral. Under her real name, Maguire, she was an immediate target.'
'They gave me my first fictitious identity when I joined in the '90s,' Blanka added as she signed onto the screen using the stylus attached to the case.

A hand-print outline displayed. With Blanka's right hand in the outline, another message flashed

*Bronwyn Mary Brown — CIA Executive Field Chief,
NATO agent U4 — verified*

Realizing that Blanka needed to be alone, Adele and Commander Gray withdrew to the door. Once there the commander whispered to Adele, 'And *Blanka?*'

'Her stepfather, Professor Hart, along with Dr. Oxberry – the geniuses behind the OhZone program – they came up with that nickname,' Adele whispered. Gray nodded.

Waiting only to take a deep breath, Blanka pressed a button marked proceed. The short letter appeared on Central Intelligence Agency letterhead. Signed by her mentor, CIA Director Admiral Keith De Leon, it read

Re. Metapox Vaccine

Dear Executive Field Chief Brown,

I briefed President Obama an hour ago in the presence of the Secretary for National Intelligence and the Secretary for Defense. Your OhZone initiative to create a Metapox Vaccine is approved. Budget details and restrictions, if any, will follow.

The President has obtained from President Higgins of Ireland agreement to grant asylum to Major Grinin and his family effective 72 hours from the time of this communiqué. OhZone will be responsible for their long-term security once they reach Dublin.

If you cannot obtain MI6/UK Gov agreement regarding the Vaccine, Commander Gray who accompanies this Defcon, will liaise with you over the options available after the 72 hours time frame has been met.

3.3

C's Jaguar, though not up to James Bond standards – it had no reflective-sensor invisibility screen, twin machine guns, or guided missile system – was nevertheless bullet-proofed and on the consul beside him was an ʊScanner C had appropriated from OhZone. As he sped his F-type east along the south coast motorway (the M27) the Scanner's number plate recognition system displayed the reassuring message

You are not being followed

The snow, still pristine in the fields, was piled up in lumps of brown slush on the edge of the carriageway. The majority vote in favour of Blanka's plan for a vaccine had caught him off guard. Russia had outmanoeuvred him and it rankled. The Russia Desk and OhZone, on Floor 12 of headquarters, were the twin banes of his life. The elevator stopped at 12 and he had to face them every time he descended from his penthouse office suite and private dining room. He dialled on the car's mobile, and a woman's voice answered. He pressed a sequence of scramble buttons. 'Secure?' he said.
'Yes,' answered Felicity. 'I'm watching Grinin eat his tea.'
'Yes, *Sir*,' snapped C. Felicity was in the blacked-out back of an unmarked Ford van parked on the River Thames embankment. The monitors in front of her showed Major Grinin, Diana and their two daughters sitting at a table while their Russian Nanny served dinner. C had caught Felicity in the middle of chatting to the male techie while applying Vaseline to her lips, which were full but dry. She put the Vaseline down next to her make-up mirror and big Bulgari sunglasses.
'Rumour has it Blanka got the better of you,' Felicity said.
'Lose the battle, win the war,' said C. 'I want you to back off. Blanka's

going to be moving in.'
'Back off for Blanka?! I thought –'
'Follow orders. I'll brief you at 14:00 hours Friday. Out.'
Felicity pulled off her Comms headset in disgust and slammed her fist on the consul.

C was devious, amoral and opportunistic, but he possessed a philosophical attitude to setbacks that made him a great survivor. Perhaps it was because there was little in the world he truly valued. The instinct for self-preservation, common to everyone, was his default setting and he had it in greater measure than most. The altered situation required a rapid readjustment of his plans. He drove past the warships anchored in the Solent, a sight he always found comforting.

C's spirits were considerably restored by the time he turned into Queens Road towards his out-of-town office near Brighton train station. He looked at the South Downs behind the town, their tops lost in icy mist and the lights on the slopes below them shrouded in haze. The newsreader on BBC Sussex informed him that the Foreign Office had definite proof Russian agents were behind the attempted assassination, earlier in the year, of Nobel Prize winner Major Grigori Grinin.

The elevator brought C up to the ground level foyer. From a curved teak reception desk facing the glass frontage, a smartly uniformed female security guard greeted him, 'Good evening, Sir Tony.'
'Good evening, Christine. I'm going straight up.'
'Dad's put ice in your office for the Caol Ila.'
Back in the elevator he inserted a digital micro key into the control panel and turned it. When he pressed the top button for the fifth floor, the display light registered the number six. Carrying a

burgundy leather briefcase bearing crown insignia, C emerged onto floor 6, which was empty and appeared to be undergoing redecoration. Opening a fire alarm panel to reveal a keypad, he inserted his micro key and entered a six-digit code. A maintenance door clicked open a few inches.

Beyond it, in front of a massive steel door, C went through the ritual at a palm, retina, and voice recognition sensor. Satisfied on all points, the sensor bade him welcome and the door softly whooshed open.

The antique Napoleonic leather-topped desk in C's private office commanded views east and west along the coastline. On a clear day you could see the Isle of Wight (though not Jersey). In front of Brighton's stylish Regency architecture, rose the revolving tower of the 'British Airways i360', described by its supporters as a space age capsule ascending to the skies. But architecture was the last thing on C's mind. He had invested a lot of time on his plans for disposing a British supply of Metapox, and he needed to find a way to prevent Major Grinin from producing the vaccine.

Opening his burgundy briefcase, he threw down a pair of government issue manila square cut folders (color: buff). They were labelled 'ʊ7' and 'Major G. Grinin' respectively. Felicity's photograph protruded from the one, but C opened the other and carefully spread its contents on his desk, with a photograph of the Major on top. He dropped two cubes of ice into a whisky glass before half filling it from a bottle of Caol Ila 1999 and adding water from a ceramic jug. Sipping his single malt and wreathed in the smoke of his embargo-busting Cuban cigar, C considered his options.

His eyes wandered to the Hologram-Comms-link set up in the far corner, a device reserved for communications between himself and **one other person**. He felt his anxiety increase.

Seeking a distraction C turned his mind to the evening ahead. He wouldn't change here, he would take an overnight bag and shower at the hotel. Opening his black Dunhill attaché case, he set it on a side table and turned to his safe. Confident in his outer security measures, C's wall safe had only a twin tumbler combination and was hidden in the first place anyone would look: behind the hinged portrait of Queen Elizabeth the Second. He took out one of the five-gram plastic bags of cocaine resting beside a red Bonham's diamond case.

As he put the cocaine into the Dunhill case, his mind flashed to his altercation with Blanka at the conference. Like mother like daughter, he couldn't help thinking. I don't see any blood, she says, the bitch. But you will see it, I promise.

He looked at the date on the bottle – Caol Ila 1999.
A good year, he thought. The year the bitch's mother died.
He returned to the safe and reached deep inside to a bottom shelf packed with manila square cut folders (color: blue). He flipped through the folders until he came to one marked *Operation Fatima*.

At his desk he opened the file. He knew the contents well. The first page was a black and white photograph, a 'corpse shot'

> *Dead woman, mid-thirties, pretty. On an ambulance gurney with her wet dress stretched tight over her. Her swollen breasts and abdomen clearly showed she was near the term of her pregnancy. The top corner of the photograph was marked 'Kitty Maguire'*

The photograph didn't show the color of Kitty's dress, but she'd been wearing blue, C remembered.
'An admiral's daughter who acted like white trash,' C said to himself. 'She had it coming.'

'You can't stop the Fatima Secret,' Kitty had told him, 'I told Major Grinin.'

C smiled. How wrong she was. I will stop it – by killing two birds with one stone.

The photograph of Kitty's body was struck through with a red line and stamped across the bottom also in red. The letters on the stamp spelled 'Terminated,' and were followed by the following words, in flowery handwriting

Vatican City, 1999: Operation Fatima

A bold pre-emptive action had served him well in that case, and it would serve him well now.

He walked to his stationery cabinet, taking out a fresh manila square cut folder (color: blue) and a red marker pen.

Grinin's fate was sealed.

C returned to his desk. 'I need a name,' he said thoughtfully. He drained his glass, stubbed out his Cohiba Lancero cigar and slid Grinin's mugshot towards himself. He aligned a ruler across his face and struck through the image in red. Then he wrote *with his left hand* in the same flowery handwriting

Operation Penthouse

The ink was black. There wasn't a drop of green anywhere ℧

The Judgement of Blanka

*This is the most horrible crime ever committed
in the whole history of the world*

JULY 1944, PRIME MINISTER SIR WINSTON CHURCHILL, UPON
READING THE FIRST DETAILED ACCOUNT OF AUSCHWITZ

Thursday. 8:20 a.m.
Secret Intelligence Service, Vauxhall Cross, London S.E.1

Secret Intelligence Service, so many names for lies, thought
C, as he hurried out a rear door of MI6 and it started to drizzle on
him. What a long winter, he reflected, as he looked at the remnants
of the snow. He turned a corner and descended steps two-at-a-
time to the Thames where the thick London fog was rolling in
off the chill river. When C was younger, it had been called a 'pea-
souper'. He kicked a lump of frozen snow off the bank and into the
water. It fizzed weakly as it was engulfed by the billows of fog. The
intolerable damp made him shudder. He'd been a director and
now head of MI6. He'd worked his way to the top, tooth and claw.
Years it had taken him and he still had to deal with the petty, dirty
details. How much longer must he endure this? Changing his
thoughts to a happier topic he remembered the evening before
with a smile. He'd enjoyed his night in Brighton and decided to
get a train up as he hadn't had his driver there. But the train ran

late. As he remembered the foggy view of The Shard, while stuck outside London Bridge Station, the smile vanished. Why hadn't he booked a helicopter? Now he was late. What was the point of having a helipad and not using it? He glanced at his watch anxiously as he scurried along the river bank.

Half an hour later, C sat glumly at an easy chair and table in the 'safe room' within his apartment. An Archimedes cage, impenetrable to ℧Scanners and surveillance by Blanka or anyone else. The Hologram-Comms-link retained a faint after-glow of its activity and its words still stung him. 'You too old for this? If you can't control Felicity,' the voice had warned him, 'It'll be on your head.' He gritted his teeth and stared at the vacant hologram.

Casa Blanka, 10 Buckingham Mews, S.W.1

*B*lanka's old fashioned pink kettle whistled. It complemented her kitchen where sculptures of endangered animals in a wall-to-wall rainforest were animated by her sampled mix of the piano and drums intro to *Love, Reign o'er Me*. It was quintessentially Blanka: a little bit of The Wild in the midst of S.W.1. Blanka peeked out a back window onto what the English called a cottage garden and beyond that to her orchard and beehive. My bees are huddled like a rugby scrum, she thought, as her vision penetrated the fog. She loved to see shapes of animals in the trees and she fancied that behind her English oak the fog made the shape of a fire dragon. On the sill inside sat herbs, stones and figures laid out in a Zen herb garden; a Buddha sat in the *relationship corner*.

On her mix CD, Jack Nicholson's voice rang out from *Live Aid* at South Philadelphia's rock-icon J.F.K. Stadium

Got a big surprise coming up for you from Wembley. Here's a truly legendary rock 'n' roll band, please welcome The Who

'That was how your mother got the nickname *J.F.K.*,' Blanka's grandmother had explained. 'As they were busy gunning down the young president, America's new hope, Kitty was busy being born. She told me it reminded her what happened to people, no matter what they did or how *good* they were.' Blanka swallowed hard at the memory. 'Maybe she saw it coming. I still remember Billy's words. He was a very tough man, but he was white. He held Kitty and kissed her. "Jane," he said. "They've assassinated the President."'

Blanka selected a box of tea from the cupboard. The sounds of piano, cymbals and rain mixed with the kettle clicking off. 'One for each person and one for the pot,' she said, as she spooned two tea-spoonful of Lapsang Suchong into the pot. She reached into the Zen garden and lifted up a pink envelope addressed to Miss Emma and Miss Olga Grinin. She took stamps from a drawer and stuck the face of Queen Elizabeth the Second onto the envelope. Her eyes turned to the *Moon calendar* Nearby had given her for Christmas. March: Pisces the fish. In the square for Sunday she had written, 'Emma & Olga are 3!' Today was circled in red crayon: red for blood, her blood. 'Dialysis,' it said.

I never used to dream, she told herself. I just saw angels when I slept, it always seemed that way. The calendar read: 'Moon in Sagittarius conjunct Saturn. Guilt about the past needs to be overcome. Challenging issues or memories relating to distant family.' The Who song came to the lines, 'Only love can bring the rain / That falls like tears from on high.' It made her want to cry, she didn't want to cry. She pressed the stop button. Her kitchen grew quiet.

When the 'Blanka' CD stopped spinning, the top looked like this

She re-boiled the kettle and poured the water into her China tea pot. As she stirred the tea, the leaves filled the water, turning it an opaque brownish-red. It was the color of dried blood, she thought. She struggled to remember something she'd promised her mother (Blanka was haunted by her memories of her mother: in ways she could barely acknowledge) – it was to do with the date of the Live Aid concerts, July 13th... 7/13 – Oh that date in 1917, thought Blanka, when the *Fatima Secret* was given to little Lucia and her cousins. It was in Kitty's papers, what needed to be done with her Fatima stuff

Her Fatima box

She went to her parlour and rummaged through the under-the-stairs cupboard. She found other stuff of her mother's but she couldn't find her Fatima box. 'It's definitely somewhere,' she said. Then her eyes settled on her Christmas decorations box. She opened it and lifted out an antique set of Christmas angel chimes, wrapped in yellowed tissue paper. She turned the bronze angels over in her fingers. She'd had the angel chimes fifteen years. They'd come from *Auschwitz*. Something beautiful from such horror. 'They belonged to the German Cardinal who befriended your mother,' her stepfather had told her. 'She wanted you to have them.'

While the tea steeped, Blanka arranged the chimes on their delicate mounts and spun them around by hand. She stared entranced as the five angels whirled on their wings, sung ever-so-softly and carried her mind drifting back.

She remembered that Christmas evening with Sokol three months before when the chimes had hung over her Christmas tree. Two red candles coaxed the angels into spinning serenely, their trumpets making the sweetest sounds as they struck the chimes. A log fire blazed in her hearth and her black cat Luna watched from the sofa as Sokol stood beside the tree with her dog, Puppy, at her feet. People regarded Blanka as an oracle, a Solomon-like woman whose judgements were infallible. Sokol had always shared these views. Until Christmas, until the marriage of Felicity-fast-track. Now Felicity-OhZone. How *could* she have let it happen?

Felicity's first nickname was Felicity-from-the-mailroom. She had a way of delivering the mail that suggested other abilities and the willingness to use them, and she soon attracted the attention of C. When he promoted her to field agent, then Grade 3 and finally 4, it was generally assumed he had more uses for Felicity than just sex. They liked using each other – for sex, for power – it didn't matter, it was all the same. And they liked destroying things; wrecking people, Blanka's key OhZone lieutenants Sokol and Crusoe. Two years back, when Sokol and Crusoe Robinson were to be married, they made breaking them up part of their plan to subvert OhZone. C had a note forged in the MI6 laboratory in Crusoe's handwriting – asking Felicity to meet him 'for some fun' – and waited for the bachelor party. Felicity was a powerful charmer: strong and persuasive as well as attractive. She spiked Crusoe's drink at his stag night and managed to haul the Australian ♂agent into a janitor's office at the venue and get his pants down. After blowing him hard she arranged for a hurried act of copulation, with Crusoe on top; to be discovered by three of his Australian friends who C had orchestrated to go looking for him. Crusoe could barely remember anything from that night. But Felicity had the forged note. From C's perspective, it destroyed an important OhZone alliance and dealt a body blow to all his American enemies. They hit us all, Blanka told herself: me, Max Hart, Dr Oxberry, Admiral De Leon and even Don Fox, the Foreign Office chief psychiatrist who, for some reason, C considers his archenemy. But that wasn't enough. C and Felicity then targeted Russia and the Russia Desk. Felicity went after Crusoe's younger brother (and Russia's rising star and right-hand-man) Jude. Her seduction of him completed, their wedding date was set for January.

Felicity loved destroying people. Torpedoing the hope of one marriage, and then entering another to bring a second good man down. With a bitterness she'd only experienced once before, the bouncy lyrics from a Simon and Garfunkel song echoed in Blanka's head. It was called *Mrs. Robinson* and it applied as well to Felicity Robinson as it did to the Mrs Robinson of the 1967 film it came from, *The Graduate*. Jesus. Heaven. Prayer.
Sokol standing near the Christmas tree looking at a spot on the wall. Once again Blanka saw the pain in her face and heard it in her voice. 'Felicity destroyed Crusoe and ruined my life. Now she'll be Mrs-I-fucked-Agent-Robinson-*Number 2*.' Then came the words Blanka would never forget. 'Blanka, it has to be done. I must *kill her* before she kills Jude.'

Sokol was red bloodied and vengeful, and as ℧5 she could have easily torn Felicity limb from limb. A clean hit (at which the KGB, MI6 and ℧ were so proficient) would leave nobody any the wiser. Sokol didn't care if the round was 7.2mm, 9mm or forty-five as long as it went between Felicity's eyes. In fact she was going to wait till Felicity was drunk on her hen night and throw her to her death from her hotel balcony. Blanka fought with her memories: 'Don't make me go through that again,' she whispered to herself. Or was she talking to Sokol? But she could still see how Sokol had knelt before her in the glow of the angel chimes and the small pale lights of the Christmas tree. The angels sung their perfect harmony and Puppy whined and licked her face, as Sokol laboured to explain.

'Don't you see? There is no God and I no longer have a country or a church. You are my country and my church. I need your approval.' Blanka had never seen tears in Sokol's eyes before and knew it was a speech she had been preparing for a long time.

'Get up, Sol, please get up,' Blanka said, pulling Sokol to her feet. 'We're friends, we're equals,' she continued.

'Friends, yes,' said Sokol. 'But we're not equals. You're good. There's nothing in your heart but goodness. But I must *act* before she kills again.'

'But she kills for *us*, just like *you* kill for us,' Blanka had insisted.

'You know that's not the *only killing* she's done,' Sokol told her.

'We don't have proof,' Blanka had replied and then regretted it.

Sokol was silent and then gripped Blanka's shoulders. 'She is CCU-8 with a trail of dead bodies behind her.'

Blanka shook her head, 'I don't believe it. Women are not capable...'

Sokol seemed to become intent on the angels and the beautiful sound they made. Then she reached out and stopped their turning. 'How *can* you believe there's good in everyone? Just look at *us*. Think about what *we do*.' She took her hand away from the chimes. Blanka blinked. 'I think about it every single day, Sol. When a body's found in the woods, when I hear how many we've killed protecting democracy. When I look at my face in the mirror. When I look at the anguish on my priest's face, on the other side of the confessional.'

In her heightened anxiety, Blanka had unconsciously started her deep breathing exercises, which so disconcerted Puppy that he started a half whine, half bark. Blanka had squatted down to comfort him. Sokol had laughed and squatted too, scratching his ears. 'Why are we arguing?' she'd said. Then, stroking Puppy, 'You don't understand, do you?' She turned back to Blanka, having recovered and become the familiar Sokol, resolute and quietly ironic.

'Why are you still in this business? The truth is you prefer animals to people. Christ knows you don't need the money! Why don't you just help your animals? Your simple, *uncomplicated animals?*'

*F*or twenty years Blanka had repeated the mantra *there is good in everyone* while serving two countries, one church, one world (as she saw it) and NATO as the West's most respected field Intelligence officer. At times she was convinced that two decades of fear and doubt had taken such a toll on her kidneys that they had some how shrivelled up to the point that dialysis was required. But that was something she would never confess to anyone.

Blanka returned to her kitchen, set the angel chimes down next to the teapot, fitted the tea strainer on her dolphins cup and saucer, and poured the dark tea through it. She took a matching milk jug from her pantry, poured in the milk, stirred the tea and took a big sip of the smoky Lapsang Souchong. Pulling a packet of McVities Rich Tea biscuits from the cupboard, she sat down, took out several biscuits and dunked the first one absent mindedly into her tea. When she finished the biscuit, Blanka flicked on a Marshall valve amp hiding under the table and lifted up her Leo Fender Precision bass guitar. She picked out a thundering bass riff from the middle of Al Stewart's long *Roads To Moscow* and sang

> *Two broken Tigers on fire in the night*
> *Flicker their souls to the wind*

But her mind was still full of that awful night with Sokol. She couldn't stop thinking about it. Sokol had warned Blanka that if Felicity lived, married and then went on into OhZone, The Machine in Paris, *The Machine that saw all*, would prove her right. Blanka feared and hated the OhZone Machine, and her resolve had hardened. She would never forget that moment of silence when Sokol turned away and touched the angels on their chimes for the last time. When she faced Blanka again, Sokol's eyes were damp but her face was deadly stern. 'You must decide. I will abide by your decision,' she'd softly said.

In place of murder, Blanka suggested a 'gesture of revenge.' Ten weeks ago, to the day, Felicity had married Jude in a beautiful white wedding dress. With only a discrete scorch hole through the back of her veil to show how very close she had come to her execution.

To escape those memories Blanka cued a YouTube video of her and Sokol playing *Roads To Moscow* in happier days. The ten-year-old recording showed Blanka and Sokol on a Thames river barge looking up at Tower Bridge and Blackfriars Rail Bridge as they sailed west. Blanka watched herself thunder out the haunting bass line as Sokol sings

> *We wait in the lines for the final approach to begin*
> *It's been almost four years that I've carried a gun*

The cat flap flew open and Luna ran in followed by wisps of fog. She meowed at Blanka and ran upstairs. Blanka set down her Fender, grabbed another Rich Tea and trotted after her.

As Blanka followed Luna into the bedroom the cat jumped on to the bed. Blanka looked across it at her wardrobe. Beside it stood the form of the life size manikin of her namesake, cousin and hero: Valentina, the only woman in the world to enter space before 1983. The manikin wore real space clothes and the first ever 'space mission patch' was sewn on the breast of its spacesuit

HISTORY PATCH #1: 1963 A.D.
Valentina went where no man had gone before

No astronaut wore a Mission Patch until Valentina

She designed and handmade the first, orbited the Earth 48 times (bearing the olive branch of peace) and stayed in space longer than the total of all previous (male) U.S. astronauts added together

Blanka munched the Rich Tea biscuit. She could still hear the music coming from the video downstairs

At home, it will almost be spring
The flames of the Tigers are lighting the road to Berlin

I wonder if Valentina knows about the Metapox Vaccine? thought Blanka as she swallowed the last of the biscuit. She couldn't very well ask her. She was now the General in charge of the Moscow Oblask KGB. She bit her lip. Did they know about it? And what would Valentina do about Grinin?

*B*lanka crept past her study, putting off her dialysis and went back downstairs. She looked out the window into her yard: if anything the fog is getting thicker she thought. She picked up the packet of non-chocolate biscuits and read the label

McVities Rich Tea Biscuits Calories and Nutrition per Serving
(1 Serving = 1 Biscuit / 8.4g)

Calories 36   Carbohydrate 5.7g of which Sugar 4.2g
Protein 0.6g   Fat 1.2g   Fibre 0.2g   Alcohol 0g

Feeling the need for chocolate, she took a packet of Lindors from the table drawer, opened it, unwrapped a handful and fed them into her mouth. At that moment her landline rang. It was a stylish, 1990s turquoise. Blanka preferred landlines since she discovered running an iPhone used more energy than running a fridge freezer. Ironically, they were also less easy to bug than mobiles. She answered it. 'Herro,' she chomped.

'Busy?' the voice at the other end said. It was Sokol.
Blanka gulped down the chocolate and hid the packet. 'No, just having a cuppa.'
'You sound funny. An American saying to a Russian: Just having a cuppa. I can taste the Lindors.'
'Cookies,' said Blanka.
'Sounds like chocolate to me. Put them away.' After a pause, Sokol asked, 'Did you get the link I sent you? The Arabian Sand Cat?'
'Thanks, it's gorgeous.' Blanka took a breath and spoke the code words, '*Love the postcard. Bye for now.*' She hung up the phone, put ℧Scanner earphones into her ears and looked at the state of Operation Russian Caravan (named by her after Grinin's favourite tea).

It was not unheard of for the US and the UK to have conflicting strategic goals. But it didn't usually happen over Weapons-of-Mass-Destruction. The British P.M. had no idea what was going on, but if C won out, the Op would see Grinin disappear from the P.M.'s own doorstep and rendered to safety in Dublin.

On her Scanner, Blanka could see the otherwise peaceful Victoria Embankment. Sokol tilted the picture up eight floors to Grinin's penthouse. Then she swung it around to show her and Puppy in a car with a British Asian agent called Krishna. They waved cheerily at Blanka. .

Crusoe's Australian voice chipped in. 'I'm on the roof, enjoying the lovely London air. Roof and airspace clear – apart from the nitrogen dioxide. No chopper will get Felicity in this way. I could do with relieving at some point today: would be nice to take a shower, remind myself what my house looks like.'

Krishna nodded to Sokol, opened the car door and climbed out.

'I know, we're short staffed,' replied Blanka. 'Hans is off to Paris to become OhZone 8 in a week. Let's concentrate on moving Grinin.'

'Krishna's on his way to relieve you,' said Sokol.

'Copy that. I'm out,' Crusoe replied.

'How are you?' It was Sokol again.

'Fine,' replied Blanka.

'You don't sound it.' Blanka could hear the concern in Sokol's voice and the sound of her taking a deep breath. 'I'm worried about the Op. We could be underestimating C.' After another pause, Sokol continued, 'And *Felicity*.'

Sensing the tension between them, Blanka remained silent, waiting. Sokol broke the silence. 'I don't want an argument with you now, but Grinin keeps disabling the bugs,' she said. 'We need someone in his penthouse around the clock. Maybe a soufflé cook, we know how he loves fine dining.'

Blanka chuckled. So Sokol was running the Op now? But it was a good idea. 'Make it so,' Blanka said. 'I'm out, unless there's anything else?'

'No. Nothing.' There was silence again, a silence full of things unsaid. Then Sokol whispered, 'Take care. We all need you. We need you very badly' – then the Scanner went black.

*B*lanka had reached the point where she could no longer put off the dialysis. The heating was up high in *Casa Blanka* as she stripped to her intimate apparel. Blue. She chose it to make her feel good. But she wasn't feeling good. Her head was slumped on her shoulder, eyes closed. She had been going to confession and mass irregularly, but now three times a week she knelt in her study for her own private act of worship: a communion of blood given and blood received. A merging with the divine, a sharing of Christ's blood; the machine took away her old blood, high in urea levels and poisoning her (like her sins, she believed) and gave her absolution, resurrection, new life. But there was a price to pay – the dream that was a relentless by-product of her exchange with the dialysis machine. Her body plugged in, her unwilling spirit returned to the nightmare of World War Two.

It usually began with a white rose of five petals, resembling the *Rose alba* of the house of York, over the door of her house. There was the friendly smell of pine trees and mountains. Somewhere a harmonica played, but all too soon the harmonica's melody was replaced by the sound of scraping. Scraping and screeching, the sound of screaming of metal. Swords and long knives being sharpened. Then Blanka would see the steel swords pushing wheels – steel against steel, spinning in endless circles. The spinning swords turned into train wheels, the sound became the unmistakable screeching of train wheels on rails.

She was riding through fog, on Caesar, who galloped next to an old-fashioned steam train which rushed through a pine forest pulling cattle trucks. There was humming, then folk guitar. Scattered among the pine trees were goats. From the first car Blanka heard the sweet, clear voice of a girl [the girl she had not yet met, Leila from Bosnia]. She was singing another Simon and Garfunkel song Blanka knew, *America*, about a girl on a bus (was she called Kitty or Katya?) looking for America. The lyrics echoed between the trees and made Blanka smile: the moon rising over lovers, fortunes and emptiness, cigarettes and pies, New Jersey and spies...

Then came the sickly smell. Blanka wanted to escape from it but she couldn't. The trees changed: they became a birch forest now and it was snowing. Barking dogs made of wire, of living steel, were shepherding the train into the railroad sidings to rest (but was it to rest?) The snow was thick on the ground as Caesar galloped closer. Suddenly, Blanka saw *her mother*. Pursued by German Shepherd dogs, Kitty was running alongside the train, trying to open the door of the second boxcar. As she struggled with the lever, the dogs caught her and pulled her down into the snow. Blood from her mother's open mouth spattered the snow crimson in the shape of a heart. Somewhere a bell tolled. The girl had stopped singing. Her song replaced by the music of Samuel Barber's *Agnus Dei*, rising, soaring. In the last truck, the one her mother was trying to open, Blanka saw two eight-year old girls, *twins*, sitting amid the straw on the floor. The huge wooden boxcar was empty except for the twins. Their pretty blonde hair was cropped. They wore the clothes that seemed at the core of her nightmares:
those smocks, *those* pyjamas

*Blanka recognized her twin cousins from Starikova family photos — Valentina's older sisters, **Katya** and **Elsa**, butchered at Auschwitz in 1944*

Then Blanka heard Caesar neighing. But she could also see – feel? – a hospital band around her left wrist. There was the humming sound, like bees, and it was snowing crystals and flakes that moved erratically, but she wasn't on Caesar anymore; she was hooked up to her dialysis machine. The train, its steel wheels spinning furiously, disappeared slowly into the crystal-fog. She became aware of Grinin standing next to her, in Red Army battle dress, a red star on his peaked officer's cap. He leaned against the machine, rubbing the stump of his arm with his good hand.

'Snow hides everything, covers all the traces,' he said in a whisper. 'I have to find my mother!' she shouted back at him as she turned to the girls who were now standing in the railway car. 'Katya! Elsa!' 'Your move,' he replied.

She was riding Caesar again, through a blizzard, galloping after the train. *She had to stop the train.* She watched Caesar's hooves rushing over a single pair of rails. The trees changed again; now they had gnarled branches. Chestnut trees and Lombardy Poplars. The branches started twisting and somehow turned into barbed wire. The scraping screaming metal sound returned. The train whistled. The sickening smell was overwhelming. The words of the *Agnus* swept her high into the sky as if on a torrent of pain

Agnus Dei, qui tollis peccata mundi, miserere nobis.

She looked down on a long line of cattle trucks. Thousands of people – in ragged, dirty coats – were reaching out their arms. Somehow, though she couldn't see, she knew there were children there. Were Katya and Elsa there?

She patted Caesar's neck to encourage him. Faster, faster. But when she looked at her hand it was covered with white powder: Caesar was turning to snow. In a sudden panic, she knew he would die. She had to stop riding. She had to walk with him. Keep him from crumbling.

Blanka walked with Caesar as he struggled against his transformation. Icy clouds came from his nostrils – and mixed with smoke from the train – then, in a moment, he crumbled away. Somewhere, again, a bell tolled.

She stared at the mound of snow which had once been Caesar. A train clanked and whistled, and she turned around. In an endless world of cattle cars – one was larger than the rest – a giant wooden horse dozens of feet high. Waffen-SS soldiers opened the side of the wooden horse and the people from the train fell out. Some were stiff like corpses, but others moved. All on top of one another they tumbled out into the snow. With Samsonite suitcases. With coats, children, dead babies.

As those who could move struggled, they turned to icy statues. Then, as the wind swirled around them, they flattened into monochrome cut-outs that trembled in the gusts of snow. They were turning to snow as Caesar had turned to snow. She had to stop them crumbling. 'Katya! Elsa!' screamed Blanka at the top of her voice.

The cut-outs, thickly covered with rags and dirty snow, rose from the pile near the train and began to move – their arms held out to her

Agnus Dei, qui tollis peccata mundi, miserere nobis.

She had to walk with them.

She ran into the crowd, but when she touched one of the women, her head fell off and she shrank to a mound of snow.
'Snow hides everything, covers all the traces,' Grinin's voice whispered again.

(For a moment Blanka got out of the dream. She was on dialysis; she could see her study around her. 'I've got to get off this machine,' she said to herself.)

Then she heard a woman laughing loudly; Blanka turned and was back in the snow.

The woman wore a white doctor's coat over a green Waffen-SS uniform, the visor cap of a Waffen-SS captain on her head. The woman was *Felicity*.

'Where's Katya?' Blanka shouted. 'Where's Elsa?'

Felicity reached up her hand and peeled a *prosthetic mask* off her face. Underneath the mask was the face of a fine-featured man of thirty, with a gap in his teeth.

Felicity with the man's face was holding the twins, hugging and swinging them.

'Who are you? What are you doing?' Blanka found herself shouting.

'*Zwillenge*,' sang Felicity happily.

Blanka fell to her knees and vomited on the snow. When there was no food to come up she vomited bile. It made a heart shape on the snow.

Felicity-man-face, Katya and Elsa under her arms, ran towards the dirty dark quarter-world of snow at the edge of the dream. Everything was gone except the black snow; there were no cut-outs, no trains or tracks. Nothing. Then in the distance, a hideous bleached glow. A huge iron Gate.

Blanka could see Katya pathetically clutching her left ear, the only color, the crimson blood running from it.

Grinin was running ahead of Blanka, trying to catch up with Katya who was reaching back to him, howling for his help. 'I have to save the children,' he yelled, as he lurched through the snow towards Felicity-man-face.

Felicity-man-face turned and pulled the children out of his reach – and smiled as Grinin *crumbled into snow*.

'*Cropped but not shaven,*' she laughed, as she pulled the twins under The Gate.

> *Lamb of God, who takes away the sins of the world, have mercy on us.*

Suddenly Blanka could see her band set up inside The Gate. She saw herself playing her Fender bass; Will was drumming, Dr Fox playing keyboard. They were performing to an audience of cardboard cut-outs: C and other spies and politicians. The band logo on the bass drum read *Point Blanka* over a telescopic gun sight. The Dream-Blanka stopped playing. She looked at Blanka and pointed. She indicated the cut-outs and another guitar propped up in the snow. The band wasn't complete.
Where was Sokol? Blanka asked herself. Where was Sokol?

As she spoke the words, Blanka could see Sokol, in 1940s clothes and make-up, run out of a door from a building labelled 'Block 24', right behind The Gate. A steel chain hung around her neck, decorated with the words

> *Arbeit Macht Frei*

just like The Gate.
Sokol plugged in her guitar and launched into the last verse of The Animals' *House of the Rising Sun* [another 1964 hit]

> *Well, I got one foot on the platform*
> *The other foot on the train*
> *I'm goin' back to New Orleans*
> *To wear that ball and chain*

'Don't you see her?' screamed Sokol, pointing at Felicity-man-face who was now fleeing through a crowd of cut-out soldiers.
She dragged Katya and Elsa along behind her on chains, their hands manacled like slaves.

Sokol looked into Blanka's eyes. She took a Russian Gyurza pistol from her belt, thrust it into Blanka's hand and closed Blanka's fingers around the trigger. 'It has to be done,' she whispered in her ear, 'She has to be stopped.'

Blanka ran through the snow. Searching. Searching. She came to a barracks. It was locked. She kicked in the door and ran inside.

Ghostly cobwebs. Hundreds of derelict bunks. Old discolored wood. It was all over. Long ago.

> Lamb of God, who takes away the sins of the world, have mercy on us.

Blanka dropped the Gyurza and fell to her knees. Sleet rained down on her through a hole in the roof. She looked up and through the hole she could see the smoke gray sky.

She heard the sound of blood pumping. Was it her blood, her dialysis machine?

It was the pumping of a child's blood. Katya's blood.

Blanka was standing in a dark corner of the barracks. In the centre she saw Katya – manacled and chained to the dialysis machine.

Naked.

Her small child's chest – cut open for surgery. Her steely blue eyes staring wildly. Everything else in the barracks was black and white like old archive film, including Katya. But her blood was red, seeping out of her chest like crimson tears

> Lamb of God, have mercy

The sound of her heart pumping

stopped.

Katya was dead. *Her eyes now empty sockets.* A hospital band was around her left wrist and her left forearm bore the black tattoo

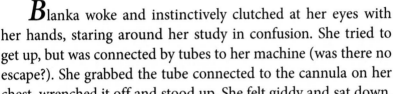

ZW – 607

*B*lanka woke and instinctively clutched at her eyes with her hands, staring around her study in confusion. She tried to get up, but was connected by tubes to her machine (was there no escape?). She grabbed the tube connected to the cannula on her chest, wrenched it off and stood up. She felt giddy and sat down. She watched her blood trickle red down her breast, falling thickly onto the mat.

She flashed back to the dream, saw Katya's blood again, and convulsed. Blood streamed out of the cannula as she struggled to cap it with the Dacron cuff. She looked down. The blood stopped. She started her deep breathing. Her hand shook violently as she cleaned herself with a wipe.

Vomit, amoeba-shaped, had hardened on the floor. So it wasn't just in the dream, she thought. The room was familiar now: her scuba tanks, masks, flippers, dive equipment and charts lay on the other side. She reached for her T-shirt and stared at the words 'Dive Master Instructor'. She almost wept at the comfort it gave her.

She pulled the T-shirt over her blue bra and sat for thirty minutes, listening to the sound of her breath.

Blanka's doorbell was an antique bell-pull connected by a cord to a string of bells. When the bells suddenly rang downstairs, she jumped. Get a grip, she thought, you're the leader of fucking OhZone, for Christ sake. She looked out the window and saw a FedEx truck parked in the Mews outside her stable door. She pulled on jogging pants, ran down the stairs and stopped in front of her cottage door. Above the hall mirror was a discrete array of security monitors. In one of them she saw the regular FedEx driver. She stared at his uniform, rubbed her face and looked in the mirror. Blanka had a lot of FedEx consignments and she'd started a light flirtation with the regular driver. I look like shit, she thought. She parted her lips and checked her teeth, grabbed a hair-band from the ledge under the mirror, tidied her hair and tied it back. Then with a big smile, she unlocked and opened the door.

'Good afternoon Magdalena,' said the FedEx man.
'Good afternoon Gary,' replied Blanka.
'To Russia with love?' he joked, tapping his PowerPad.
She looked blank. 'Your package to *Moscow*? he prompted her.
'Oh yea, sure,' said Blanka, scrambling behind the door for a small FedEx box and handing it to him.

In the kitchen, she flipped the kettle back on, picked up a pencil and wrote 'nightmare from hell' on her calendar. She'd make notes later. She picked up her Fender Precision Bass and looked at it with suspicion. In the nightmare she'd been playing it at The Gate.

The kettle whistled and Blanka jumped again. 'Fuck!' she said. The kettle bubbled and gurgled and then clicked off.

She started to play the bass, slowly at first. Gradually she picked up speed until the driving beat started her soul racing and she let the music carry her as far away from her nightmare of Auschwitz as she could get ℧

Déjà Vus

Friday, March 13. 8:15 a.m.
US Embassy, Chancery Building, Grosvenor Square, S.W.1

On paper, MI6 had agreed to support making the Metapox Vaccine, but it was clear from the bugs that OhZone had in place that C had no intention of honouring the six to three majority vote by the directors.

Although evidence of a *blue-slip* hit had not yet leaked out, Blanka was already setting Operation Russian Caravan in motion. The first hurdle was the Americans, specifically the US Ambassador to Britain and the CIA bureau chief, Steven Patrick, otherwise known as Ma Baker. Blanka's discussion with the Ambassador and Ma Baker had been brief. 'The 72-hour deadline expires tomorrow,' she reminded them. 'President Obama has given this top priority.'

'Diplomatic protocol has got to be gone through,' the Ambassador explained. 'I've briefed the Irish Defense Minister and informed him of the urgency. He has agreed to meet with me and the US ambassador to Ireland on Wednesday.'
'Wednesday!' Blanka's look of disgust required no interpretation. 'I'd hate to see how long it takes it if weren't a fucking emergency.'
'The Minister was quite reluctant to meet at all,' the Ambassador replied icily, while Ma Baker looked around for interesting objects

to divert his attention. 'And I've had to clear my diary.'

As they left the Ambassador's office, Ma Baker whispered to Blanka 'Diplomats don't think in anything less than days.'
'Am I supposed to be grateful?'
'From their side, yes.'
They had reached the embassy limousine. As Blanka and Ma Baker climbed in, he handed her a sealed envelope. 'Communiqué from Langley.' As the limousine turned onto the street, Blanka opened the envelope. It was on the Director's notepaper

Re. Operation Russian Caravan.

I concur with your plans. However, do NOT render anyone until Ma Baker confirms that all diplomatic boxes have been ticked. Cdr Gray will make US military assets available if required. Budget fifty million. I suggest you also prioritize getting new OhZone recruits to counteract Felicity Robinson Ʊ7. Keith De Leon.

Ma Baker let Blanka have time to absorb De Leon's message. Finally she glanced at him and said, as calmly as she could, 'You can bet C's not going through diplomatic channels. We have to move fast.'
'And the Russians?'
'Another reason to get our collective ass into gear. Dublin better not be a boys' pissing contest.

They drove past the fountains in Trafalgar Square. Yesterday's fog had lifted and Blanka got a clear view. She was reminded of the singing fountains of Peterhof Palace, St. Petersburg. Grinin had taken a photograph of her mother there in 1999. What was it her

stepfather, Max Hart had said? 'Your mother, Kitty, was very superstitious. She didn't like Thursdays.'
Yes, she'd died on a Thursday, thought Blanka. 'Fuck it,' she said.
Ma Baker looked at her. 'We go Thursday.'
'Okay,' Ma Baker said, as Blanka returned to her thoughts.

Valentina. She had to put up with diplomats, but that wouldn't stop her acting. If I were in Valentina's shoes, what would I do? Get him out. I would use the family connection. She looked up, as if sensing something in the air. Lara.

'I've got clearance,' Ma Baker said suddenly. He had been checking his messages. 'Wasson will be your CIA liaison and Gray your military one. What else do you need?'
Blanka thought quickly, and said, 'A fifty set CIA-Blue radio link-up with mobile control to go in my stable, up-to-the-minute Intel on the KGB's position on Grinin and two dozen field agents seconded to OhZone.'
'Jesus, Blanka, this isn't the only show on in the West End.'
'I understand it may take time. But it would be very useful to have the first dozen agents this morning. Or do you think in days too?'
Ma Baker snorted. 'You can have them. I'll get replacements flown in from Warsaw.'
'Thank you.'

As the limousine crossed Westminster Bridge towards the South Bank, Blanka looked over her shoulder at the Boudica's Chariot sculpture and River Heights behind. It would be much easier to move Grinin separately from his wife and children. If she moved Grinin first, C might kidnap the others as a bargaining chip. Diana and the twins would have to be moved first.

Two helicopters were waiting as the limo pulled up by Barclays

Battersea Heliport. An Atlas helicopter, and Ma Baker's helicopter with its engine running. Blanka could see the elderly figure of the African-American physician and scientist Dr Ray Oxberry – **Drox** – standing next to the Atlas helicopter.

Ma Baker wished Blanka good luck and climbed out. After briefly greeting Drox, he jumped into his helicopter. It rose vertically from the river heliport – into the beguilingly blue sky above London.

As she approached Drox (he had been her late mother's oldest and closest confidante) Blanka greeted him with her loveliest smile. 'My knight in shining armour!'
Drox smiled back and hugged her.
'What's the plan?' he asked (in an American voice with something of a French accent).
'We set up the move for Thursday. Women and children first,' replied Blanka. 'Can you hold off putting Hans in the OhZone Machine for a couple of days?'
'Sure, send him over when you're finished.' Drox opened the rear door of the Atlas helicopter and climbed in after Blanka.

'What about Valentina?' he asked.
'I've been pondering that,' replied Blanka. 'I think she'll play the Kitty card. Which means she's going to send an asset. She can't do it herself, so it will be one of her trusted captains.'
'Lara…'
'Quite possibly. I need to get eyes at all the airports. Can you watch the Eurostar in Paris?'
'Good ol' Gare Du Nord. Happy to oblige.' He signaled to the pilot who started the aircraft's engine.
'I need to vanish for a bit, and appear to be somewhere I'm not.'
'Nearby?'
'Can we pick her up?'
Drox nodded as the helicopter lifted off. 'No problem.'

The glare from the afternoon sun momentarily filled the interior. The helicopter turned over the river, and the Thames glimmered with silver beneath them. 'One more thing,' Blanka said, touching Drox's knee. 'What have you told Max?'

'He's been very careful not to ask. And I haven't volunteered anything.'

'I need him to think I can cope,' said Blanka.

'I can't make any promises. You can't keep hiding things from him. Sooner or later…'

'Later, Drox.' Blanka patted his knee, a determined smile on her face. 'Later. When it's over.'

*L*ate that afternoon, two removals trucks blocked the view to Blanka's mews. At number 10 Buckingham Mews a horse box had been backed up against her stable. To those in the neighbourhood, it seemed Caesar had been brought back from Dorset. In reality, a CIA-Blue Comms system and its peripherals were being quickly unloaded and three CIA techies were firing it up inside the stable. Blanka had gotten her fifty set CIA-Blue radio link-up with a mobile control.

At the same time, at London City Airport, E.16, six CIA field agents met Blanka, Nearby and Drox who had just landed. In the screened-off area Drox retained there, Blanka, Drox and five of the CIA agents boarded his Cessna Citation X jet, together with a dozen CIA-Blue Comms radios (while the helicopter was seen to be refuelled). The sixth agent stayed to stake out the City airport.

When the Atlas helicopter took off, only Nearby was in it. She carried Blanka's ℧Scanner, cell phone and a passport in the name of Ruth Baldwin, a secret OhZone identity which Blanka knew had been penetrated by C's watchers at Britain's equivalent of the NSA, called 'GCHQ.' The grid at GCHQ showed the helicopter –

with Blanka in it – heading towards London's Stansted airport. When Ruth Baldwin later checked in on a Ryanair Flight to Stockholm, C would be lead into believing that Blanka was meeting with the Swedish security service

5.2

2.30 p.m.
MI6 Headquarters, 89 Albert Embankment, S.E.1

*T*he British Government and its former leaders had many secrets. Like other former great empires, its secrets lead to more secrets, endless dark tunnels which themselves lead to catacombs, where unseemly corpses lay.

Until quite recently, the government pretended MI6 only existed in the books and the films. It had no address or website or entry in the phone book. A triumph of MI6's post-cold-war dissembling was its catch phrase, 'It's really nothing like James Bond.' A beautiful piece of quantum spin, it was simultaneously completely correct and completely incorrect. Correct because there was no 'double O' program with a 'license to kill' (the internationally sought 'Cadre' of special hit agents had been put out of business by OhZone, who made far less mistakes), no Scottish orphan boy and no *one* cover company called Universal Exports. Yet at the same time it was incorrect. Everything about MI6 from its nine Roman Catholic directors down to the mailroom, was far, far more like Bond than Bond ever was. MI6's Latin motto, identical in both tooth and claw to that of the Vatican's Intelligence service, the Holy Inquisition, said it all: *Semper occultum.* 'Always hidden.'

The view from C's penthouse suite on Floor 13 included River Heights. He was looking at Grinin's penthouse through a telescope, but his mind was on Felicity. 'It'll be on your head,' he'd been told. Why *had* she been thrown out of Med School? C turned and looked at her. Felicity sat like the cat with the cream, long legs crossed, perched not on the other side of C's desk but on C's black leather sofa – showing not only bare leg, but bare thigh to within an inch of her nakedness. She gave C a lover's smile.

C picked up the ʊScanner from his desk. 'I feel like a party pooper using one of their own Scanners to listen in,' he said laughing.

'From what I've seen, it's not much of a party,' Felicity replied.

'But you're going to change all that, aren't you?'

'Just give me the chance,' said Felicity ʊ7. 'I'll see you tonight, the usual time?'

'You're a married woman, Mrs Robinson. Won't your husband be expecting you to spend the night with him?'

Felicity stood up and sauntered towards him revealing the shape of her erect nipples under her thin blouse. 'Someone has overridden the Russia Desk rotas and put him on a long series of nights.' Felicity placed C's hand on top of her breast and kissed him. Her tongue made circles around his tongue. Then she pulled away and headed for the door. C savoured the taste of OhZone 7 in his mouth.

'You've forgotten something,' he said gesturing to the manila square cut folder (color: blue) lying open on his desk. The mugshot of Grigori Grinin was struck through with red marker and 'Operation Penthouse' was written across the bottom in the flowery handwriting.

'Close the file,' said C. 'The activation code is underneath.'

Felicity closed the blue file on Grinin's face and lifted it aside. Underneath was a white envelope the size of a credit card.

'I thought I was coming round tonight.'

'Of course you're coming round. Blanka's got the whole of OhZone and half the Asia-and-Russia Desks guarding him. She'll be suspicious if she doesn't see us carrying on as normal.'

'She can see your flat? The bedroom?'

'How long have you been an OhZone?'

'Since Monday.'

'It's Friday. Catch up.'

'Queen bitch. I bet she loves to run it frame by frame when you're inside me.'

'I doubt it, there are other things going on in her life. I'm not quite sure what they are, but she has issues, I know that. She'll be watching, or someone will be watching for her.'

C sat down at his desk and picked up a note written on rice paper – in the famous green ink. 'In the meantime you're befriending Frank Ryder.' He handed the rice paper to Felicity. 'This is the address of the bar he goes to every night after work. By the way, you do remember who he is?'

'The property manager at River Heights. The man who has access to everything.'

'Access to *everything*,' echoed C looking at Felicity's legs. Felicity stuck her tongue out at him.

C looked at his Rolex watch. 'He'll be there this evening.'

'But I'm seeing you.'

'Come after. I can't spare all evening. But I'm looking forward to getting reacquainted. After our performance for Blanka, I'll decide if you're staying the night.'

Felicity stifled her impulse to slap him, instead she brushed the Operation Penthouse file across C's crotch. 'And *closing the file*?'

'When I transmit the code.'

He pressed one of the many white, black and colored keys on his old-fashioned intercom: the only ice blue key.

'Sir,' answered a woman from C's unofficial Counter-℧ Desk.

'Where's Queen Boudica?'

'On Ryanair to Stockholm as Ruth Baldwin,' answered the woman.

'Thank you,' replied C, 'I wondered when Ruth Baldwin would show up.'

He let go the intercom button and turned to Felicity. 'She's been dead ten years. Blanka recently took up the name.'

Felicity shrugged.

C punched some keys on his desktop Mac, studied the screen and moved the mouse to show Grinin's diary for the forthcoming week. 'Blanka's probably moving Grinin to Stockholm. And soon. You should pay him a call on Tuesday, before she has time to arrange anything.'

Felicity dropped the white envelope into her bag.

'No, I stand corrected,' continued C. 'It's his wedding anniversary on Tuesday. I won't deny him his last rights, a man of his age.'

Felicity rolled her eyes impatiently, 'What's wrong with Monday? Does Wonderland find Mondays inconvenient for hits, so close to the weekend?'

'The *Office!*' growled C. 'Monday's Radio 2. We can't have him not turn up at the BBC, for Christ sake. Wednesday or Thursday.' C smiled. 'You choose.'

'Are we done?' said Felicity.

'Am I still required for the orphans' fair tomorrow?' asked C.

'Have you got the Bagatelle?'

'Yes.' C started looking through paper work. 'Ask Miss Banks to come in on your way out, will you?'

Felicity had turned from C, crossed his office, and opened the first of a pair of double doors when C addressed her sharply. 'You've forgotten something else,' he said. 'A required procedure.'

Felicity gave him her standard, bored pouting look.

C wiggled his finger for her to come back over to his desk. As Felicity stepped behind it, C gave her OhZone ass a mighty slap. Tight as sprung steel, he thought. Felicity raised her eyebrows, neither shaken nor stirred; maybe just slightly turned on.

'If you did that to Blanka, she'd have your arm off.'

'But you're not Blanka.' He took the rice paper from her hand, and held it up to her mouth.

'And don't you forget it. I *made you*.'

Felicity tossed her head, cascading her long hair and looked away.

'Maybe I should say I'm remodelling you,' C said. 'From a failed Medic in the mailroom to the most physically powerful woman in the world.'

Felicity thought about 'remodelling' C by ripping his arm out of his shoulder socket. She looked down at the thick carpet and imagined the pattern his blood would make on it.

'You are my beast,' C continued, 'my little wild thing, OhZone 7.'

Felicity, eyes blazing, turned her head back and parted her lips.

C fed the rice paper between them, then returned to his paper work.

Felicity marched across the carpet, chewing sullenly.

'When you're finished, Mrs Robinson,' C said without looking up, 'Be sure to close the door behind you, not required procedure simply good manners.'

Felicity held the inner door in her hand. It was a solid hardwood-core one hour fire-door, soundproofed and cushioned on the other side. She could easily rip it off its mounting, use it as a pyre to float C's dead body down the river in flames to the Thames Estuary. And she could use the outer door for Blanka. But she decided to bide her time. She had only been an OhZone four days.

★

*T*he SFE elevator (Science Floors Enabled) descended fourteen levels and approached Basement 2. It stopped silently and the doors opened like the sound of heavy snow landing. Felicity skipped out and strode purposefully down an endless corridor. Half way along, she reached double doors to one side, labelled 'Area B 21'. She went through the ritual of palm retina and voice recognition, the screen verified her as Ʊ7, and the door opened.

Down a short corridor, outside the Bio Labs, a sandwich board read, 'No Entry. CCTV maintenance in progress.' Felicity stepped round the sign, pressed a button and waited as the airtight door whooshed open. She stepped onto the padded hermetically sealed floor of the airlock and waited for the outer door to close. When the inner door opened automatically she stepped into the empty laboratory. It consisted of a central science bench and the usual equipment of microbiology and forensics: microscopes, Bunsen burner with a hot blue flame, surgical scissors, probes, scalpels, tweezers and a stack of MI6 forensic pouches. Several apertures marked with the triple-cells Biohazard symbol opened to negative airflow cabinets, freezers and internal corridors. One led to the re-frigerated mortuary boxes and pathology lab, and another led to a Biosafety Level 4 facility containing *Yersinia pestis* (the Black Death) and vacuum and UV light decontamination rooms.

'Some do it with a bitter look / Some with a flattering word.'
Felicity jumped at the suddenness of the lines spoken so close. Bio had entered behind her. 'The coward does it with a kiss / The brave man with a sword!' As she finished she popped a black combat cap with a big red star on the front on Felicity's head, and saluted her, Soviet style. 'Welcome Comrade,' Bio roared. 'Now you are properly dressed as executioner.'
Felicity was still edgy from having been startled. 'I didn't know you were a poet,' she said as she regained her composure.

'An indulgence,' Bio answered. 'One of many, to break up the tedium.' She pulled out two stools and placed them next to each other at the science bench. Felicity looked up at the CCTV cameras. 'Off for maintenance,' Bio reassured her. 'So? Got something to show me?'
From inside her bag, Felicity lifted out the white envelope. Bio handed Felicity a scalpel from the bench and Felicity slit open the envelope, removing a smaller inner one. This envelope should have been the well-known 'blue-slip'. But instead it was black. *Black.*

What did that mean? Felicity thought in a panic. The *Black Slip* tumbled from her hand. When in her agitation she jumped from her stool to reach after it, Felicity smashed her head on the bench top. Bio helped her up and walked to one of the freezers. She returned with an ice pack and applied it to the bump on her forehead. 'Oh... your first OhZone bruise.'

Still in shock from seeing the Black Slip, Felicity's hand shook as it held the envelope. Bio looked at her and smiled again.
'It matches the cap.'
Felicity glared at Bio. 'I was expecting a blue-slip,' she said.
Bio opened a drawer, took out a blue-slip from a metal box where several used blue-slips lay, and set it down in front of Felicity. 'Like this?'
Bio's casual attitude – her contempt? – irritated Felicity, but she kept silent.
'Felicity,' said Bio affectionately squeezing her arm, 'You're OhZone 7 now.'
'They didn't talk about Black Slips.'
Bio took the Black Slip from her. 'No one talks about Black Slips, black Ops. Look, they don't exist!' With a sweep of her other hand, Bio made the Black Slip disappear. She held up her empty palms to Felicity.

Felicity clenched her fists, not surprised but very angry. It wasn't the first magic trick Bio had shown her. As Bio produced the Black Slip triumphantly from behind Felicity's ear, Felicity recalled her Saturday mornings in bed with C – and the magic tricks he showed her to punctuate their bouts of sex. Bio was fifteen years older than her. Suddenly Felicity realized that C's bedroom as well as her doctorate in microbiology had been Bio's passport onto the MI6 board of directors.

Bio held out the Black Slip to Felicity. That smile again. Felicity was ready to hit her. If she was an OhZone now, why was there still this contempt? She was used to it with C, but not Bio.

'When's activation?' asked Bio.
'Next week.'
'You'd better open it then, hadn't you?'
Felicity picked up the scalpel and slit open the black envelope.

Bio looked away as Felicity withdrew a sliver of rice paper. It was marked with a random-generated activation code known only to two people: C and the agent or operative entrusted to 'close the file' – the Intelligence service term for a *lethal hit*. The code read

 317885

Field agents were trained to memorize codes in a millisecond and swallow the evidence. But there was something about the number. Felicity stared at it and stopped breathing. Goosebumps formed on her arms as if she'd seen a ghost or had a sudden flash of déjà vu.

Her right palm flew out and she gripped her tattoo with it. Regaining control of herself, she turned the rice paper over so she couldn't see the number and folded it in half, then in half again. She placed the paper in her mouth, trying to avoid getting it on her tongue. She screwed up her face and tried to swallow. She turned pale, looked like she was going to be sick, but at last swallowed it.

'Finished?' asked Bio still with her back turned. 'We all know that *Felicity-In-Wonderland* always swallows!'

Flustered, Felicity tore the combat cap off her head, glowered at the red star on the front and hurled it in Bio's face. Bio handed Felicity a pair of tweezers. Picking up the Black Slip with them, Felicity held it out towards the Bunsen burner. But she couldn't quite reach, Bio was in the way. Felicity looked Bio in the eyes. 'You're in my sodding way,' she growled.

Bio held her ground.

'What does it mean?' demanded Felicity.

Bio smiled. 'It means, get closer to me.'

Felicity shook her head. 'Not until you tell me what it means. Why didn't I get a blue-slip?'

'You honestly don't know?'

Felicity was silent, waiting. Not getting any more she yelled, 'Tell me!'

'Dr Oxberry has been horribly lax in his training at OhZone or you don't bother to listen,' giggled Bio.

'Laugh it up,' said Felicity. Bio grinned expectantly.

'I didn't stay for the last part of the training,' admitted Felicity. 'I was bored in Paris.'

Bio roared with laughter. 'You were *bored in Paris*? Perhaps we *should* have made Nearby the OhZone.'

Felicity slammed both Bio's arms to the bench with her right hand. 'Don't make me hurt you,' she hissed between her teeth.

Bio pulled a hand free and held up the blue-slip. 'Keep this with you so the OhZones will see it. Blanka will be expecting you to have a blue-slip hit.'

Felicity took the blue-slip and squeezed herself closer to Bio so their chests pressed against each other, their lips just inches away.

She put her lips to Bio's ear and whispered, 'Tell me. With a Black Slip, what can I do?'

'It's no holds barred,' Bio said, turning and gently kissing Felicity's cheek. 'Collateral damage allowed. I hear you don't mind collateral damage in your personal life. Now you can mix business with pleasure.' Bio moved her lips to Felicity's mouth.

Felicity turned her head away. She could now reach the Bunsen burner and held the Black Slip in the flame. The Slip ignited in the centre and burned slowly outwards.

She smiled as she watched the flames engulf the paper, curling up orange black, red black red (like a Swastika, Felicity thought) then flickering yellow and incinerating.

'Does collateral damage include killing Blanka?'

'Don't be Felicity-from-the mailroom! If you kill Blanka you'll go to prison. And quite rightly so!'

Bio screwed up her face in a look of distaste: 'Women's prison! They'll poison you or put ground glass in your food. Blanka and Sokol have powerful friends. Besides I wouldn't take on Blanka. All that "there's good in everyone and I rescue wild animals" is a front. She's a ruthless killer, like you. And *a lot* more experienced.'

As she spoke, Bio lowered her head and kissed Felicity's hand as it held the now empty tweezers. 'Other than that, Black Slip means *no limits*.'

'Mm,' said Felicity.

Bio travelled quickly up Felicity's arm and kissed her neck.

'And *my list of requisitions*?' asked Felicity.

Bio gave a mock salute. 'I'm meeting her tonight, Ma'am. I'll have the two laboratories working on Saturday.'

Felicity kissed Bio's lips, and then bit her on the lip, drawing blood

5.3

*A*t Thames House, 12 Millbank, S.W.1, the Director General Capability (DGC) of Military Intelligence Section 5 (Blanka knew them as the 'Other Firm' or MI5) stood at his window also engaged in the British custom of sipping tea and trying to escape his troubles. He viewed the fog swirling on the river and the little waves lapping against the ancient stones of the Palace of Westminster with consternation.

He sat down and stared at a silver tray and sugar bowl and then at the woman sitting opposite him, the head of JTAC. 'Sweet enough?'. 'Quite,' she replied. He offered her a McVities Milk Chocolate Digestive biscuit from a plate. She shook her head, sipped her tea and glanced back down at another manila folder (color: gray). It contained a family photograph of Grinin, Diana and their twins.

'Guarding him from whom?'
'Red Russians? White Russians? Non-Russians? Hard to say really.'
He sighed as he took a biscuit. 'But we need to up security.'
'We can't up it. We don't have any on him.'
The DGC bit into his Digestive and shook his head, 'No.'
'OhZone has been doing it since he was – *shot.*'
The DGC swallowed. 'An own-goal if ever I saw one. But in this election climate, *we* are being held to blame.'
'But we weren't guarding him.'
'The P.M. wants to know why.'
'Why we weren't guarding him? "6" was doing it, he's their man!'
'He telephoned me himself, Corduroy. He described Grinin as, "a *modern-day Da Vinci*, gunned down like a common gangster, in a Westminster street," he said.'
'Are gangsters gunned down in Westminster streets? Well, this

Nobel scientist must be important! Can he read?'

'Grigori Grinin?'

'Mr Corduroy,' she said tersely, tapping the manila folder. 'The file *clearly shows* that "6" was doing it.' She blew air out between her lips, and looked at her watch. 'Budget and time scale?'

'Whatever you need and *immediately*,' said the DGC draining his tea cup and taking another chocolate biscuit.

'I'll have the Op file on your desk in an hour. Give it the green light and we'll be in there tomorrow. What do we call it?'

The DGC thought. 'Hmm let's call it, Operation Digestive.'

8.30 p.m.
Liverpool Street Station, The City of London, E.C.2

*D*uring the afternoon, at just short of Mach 1, Dr Oxberry's Citation X jet zipped him and Blanka the length of England, landing agents at Birmingham, Manchester and Newcastle, and depositing two in Scotland for Edinburgh and Glasgow airports. Others rushed to Luton, East Midlands and Bristol airports. Heathrow and Gatwick were watched by one at each terminal. Drox's jet deposited Blanka back at City Airport before returning Drox to Paris.

As night fell, Nearby, who had returned from Stockholm, came in on the shuttle train from Stansted airport on its dedicated plat-form, 7, at the main train station serving the City of London. She was to meet Blanka who would arrive on the subway, wearing a beard and passably disguised as a man.

In the briefest of encounters, she would return Blanka's Scanner and phone, effectively putting the real Blanka back on the grid, and continue with her next assignment – to watch passengers arriving from London Stansted airport.

When Nearby stepped off the shuttle train she suddenly froze as she came face to face with a large bronze public sculpture immediately opposite the ticket barrier from the platform. It was of two children from the 1930s: bronze refugees from the *Kindertransport*.

Nearby stared at one of the bronze figures – an eight year old girl. Was I like that? suddenly thought Nearby. Then an image flooded her whole being (before she came to her senses and hurried upstairs to the Foxes bookshop) a quite irrational scene – a steam train whistling, its brown smoke mixing with snow – some kind of a déjà vu

inside her mind — in a sepia 1940s photograph she, Nearby, was standing shoulder-to-shoulder with Blanka's mother, Kitty Maguire ℧

Scorns of Time

Never Did the Cyclops' Hammers Fall
On Mars's armour forged for proof eterne
With less remorse than Pyrrhus' bleeding sword
Now falls on Priam.

Out, out, thou strumpet Fortune! All you gods
In general synod take away her power,
Break all the spokes and fellies from her wheel
And bowl the round nave down the hill of heaven,
As low as to the fiends!

WILLIAM SHAKESPEARE - HAMLET

— TWENTY-SIX YEARS EARLIER —

Wednesday, December 7, 1988. 11:00 p.m. GMT
Flight PA103. Latitude 46.60° North, Longitude 36.07° West

American captain James MacQuarrie emerged from the rest room on the upper deck of the Pan Am Jumbo jet, exchanged smiles with the woman with green eyes in First Class seat 61K and passed through the doorway to the flight deck. He glanced at the four EPR gauges of the Pratt and Witney engines (1.32 each), exchanged a word with his co-pilots and slid behind the controls for the rest of the ride. The 747-121 was mid-Atlantic between Limerick where it had left behind the Irish midlands and Gander on the island of Newfoundland.

The woman with green eyes in 61K was Kitty Maguire. Twenty-five years old – Kitty thought she had her whole life ahead of her.

She glanced out her window at the ocean, cramping her neck forward, west, to see the light, the last remains of the setting sun, ahead over Canadian waters. As she gazed into the sea below, her mind travelled back five months to July – and tried to make sense of the changes. Five months ago she was flying over the North Sea – the cold cold stretch of water that separated the Isle of Britain from Germany, Scandinavia, the continent of Europe – not the Atlantic. And her destination was a windswept oil rig, not New York City, the place she felt most at home. The oil rig belonged to one of the world's biggest corporations, BP, British Petroleum. The flight had also been on a Wednesday she remembered.

Am I really going home now? she asked herself. Am I really wealthy, beyond my wildest dreams? With checking and savings accounts at Coutts in London and The Bank of New York at One Wall Street? Can I really have whatever I want?

She wanted a cigarette. She took a Marlboro Red soft pack (the American pack so hard to get in Europe) from her breast pocket and flipped a cigarette out. This deck was no smoking, she'd have to go downstairs to light it. Max was always on to her about cutting down. She tapped the cigarette on her tray table, looked out her window again and down into a sea of indigo.

*K*itty had just quit her job as a film and t.v. producer at BP.

But five months ago she had been shooting a promotional film at BP's *Fortes* oil field. Because underwater sequences were involved, Kitty had hired a special film crew led by her current boyfriend, Max Hart, who was a combination diving cameraman, medic and archaeologist. After celebrating the 4th of July ashore in Aberdeen with a large party of Americans, they had flown out early on the 5th: a three-hour trip in the cramped noisy Bristow twenty-seat helicopter. Half an hour from their destination they had passed over Occidental Petroleum's 'cash cow', a production platform, *Piper Alpha*. It was busily pumping a fortune in black gold: one eighth of the total output of the North Sea fields, not only from its own wells but from two other fields linked to it by giant feeder pipelines.

Kitty and Max had unpacked on *Fortes*, surveyed the above-the-water shooting locations and its oilfield support vessel, the *Iolair*, and liaised with the Offshore Installation Manager. They had slept on the *Iolair* while waiting for the rest of the crew and the aerial filming kit arriving the next morning, Wednesday, the 6th of July.

As she slept out there on the North Sea, on the eve of the *Piper Alpha* disaster, Kitty had had a particularly strong and vivid dream... It was not the first time she had dreamed of World War Two and Valentina's older sisters, Katya and Elsa. The family's history chronicled that they had been captured in western Russia and eventually shipped to the Auschwitz concentration camp complex. Valentina's parents ultimately survived; but Katya and Elsa – eight years old and identical twins – were consigned to the Auschwitz-Birkenau science division: Block 32 of the Gypsy Camp.

The doctor in charge there – an expert in dissembling, and obsessed with eye color – set up a kindergarten and playground for the children and had them call him, 'Uncle.'

Uncle Mengele. But there was no singing round the Gypsy-camp-fire there. The deepest burning inferno of hell was a walk in the park, compared to Block 32.

Armed with a cloak of invisibility, a winning smile, power-absolute and *bags of sweets*, Mengele abused Katya and Elsa – and other identical twins and Gypsy and Jewish children (as young as two), as well as pregnant women near term – performing bizarre surgical transplants and experiments on them, while they were fully conscious. With no nursing or anaesthesia, the children were tortured to their deaths; after which the doctor removed *their eyes*, which he pinned to his wall. Those who survived, Mengele murdered by injection or sent to the Auschwitz gas chambers.

Kitty's mother had told her how their family had been blooded by this man – the world's worst escaped *serial child killer*. It had marked one generation and all the generations that followed. Kitty fought back the tears – it had made her blood boil to hear of it, even when she was young, and she was convinced that the story of Katya and Elsa remained untold. She would have to put it to rights. Now she was wealthy beyond belief, she could make films telling the truth. The whole truth.

★

*I*n Kitty's dreams it was usually Katya whom she followed. That night Katya's dream spirit took her away from Auschwitz and revealed something quite different – and utterly wonderful.

In the dream, Katya took Kitty's hand and pulled her under the warm waters of the Aegean. They dove to the seabed and there Katya gestured for Kitty to follow. Coming to what seemed like a well shaft on the ocean floor, Katya again took her hand. She led Kitty down the shaft, a hundred feet down. In the murky water at the base of the well, Kitty saw the top of a huge rock. It was covered with barnacles that glittered in places as the water moved around it. Katya moved aside some weeds and pressed Kitty's hand against the surface of the rock. Her hand sank into it. Under inches of muck she felt metal, and she was filled with the sense of a staggering treasure thousands of years old! Katya pulled her back so she could see more clearly. As the rock glowed, the barnacles and muck-of-ages momentarily disappeared, and Kitty was left with the vision of a huge shining object – made of solid gold – in the shape of a heart.

★

Over breakfast the next morning, Kitty told Max about her dream of an 'underwater treasure' in the Aegean. It reminded him of an opening he had seen on one of his archaeological diving expeditions off the Turkish shore, and he mentioned it to Drox over the ship to shore radio. 'It's a little like relying on a divining rod to find water,' Drox replied, 'but it's worth a try.'

But later that day an underwater treasure was the last thing on Kitty's mind. Instead, she was engulfed in another fiery hell and a massive black cloud spewing from tons of burning oil. Kitty and her aerial film crew were in a helicopter some distance from the *Piper Alpha* platform when the first explosion jolted them. The crew put their cameras down and stared at the catastrophe, unable to comprehend it, while the pilot radioed the Mayday distress call. Kitty listened with incredulity as they were instructed to return to their base in the Fortes oil field.

'No,' commanded Kitty. 'Don't you dare!' The moment she saw the tiny figures below her, enveloped in their peril, she felt a fury rise up from deep deep within her. 'Film this, people need to see the truth!' In the next half hour Kitty was like a banshee – as if she were the sole force keeping the helicopter in the air, near the churning tragedy. 'Get that!' she had yelled, now pointing to one place on the stricken platform, then to another. As dozens of oil workers assembled on the helideck Kitty persuaded the pilot to fly closer to winch some off, only to have the helicopter beaten back by the rising jets of flame. As oil workers started to jump from the helideck into the ocean two hundred feet below, Kitty listened in disbelief to the radio traffic: Oxy were still pumping both oil and gas down the feeder pipes from the other fields – fuelling the towering inferno which was to slaughter three-quarters of the workers aboard.

The daughter of an admiral and a diver from an early age, Kitty was a child of the ocean and convinced those in charge to let her act as rescue swimmer to winch injured workers from the water to the rescue ship *Spartan Queen*. After an hour in the rough ocean, smelling of oil and burnt flesh, Kitty was exhausted. Her face, a pitiless dark gray, had become a mask of grief. The path of the oily sea water and tears on her cheeks, black streaks of ash. Finally with the fuel gauge heading for empty, the pilot turned east for *Fortes*. A considerable distance from the rescue vessels, Kitty spotted a body floating on the water.
'There's no movement,' said the cameraman, still filming.
'He's dead,' said the pilot, 'we have to leave him.'
'No,' said Kitty. 'We have to go down.'
The others disagreed.
'He's *somebody's son!*' insisted Kitty. 'Winch me down to his body.'

As they flew back, Kitty always remembered feeling Katya's presence with her as she cradled the corpse of the young man in her lap.

Kitty never forgot the view of *Piper Alpha* from that helicopter. Her, looking down, at a city in flames, and the men of that city going to their deaths. With 167 dead, *Piper Alpha* is the world's all-time worst oil disaster. Occidental Petroleum, 'Oxy', (despite being found to blame by the official inquiry) avoided criminal charges and paid only minimal compensation. Kitty felt sick when Oxy rose to fourteen in the Fortune 500.

A month after the *Piper Alpha* catastrophe, Max Hart and Drox returned to the Turkish coast and explored the hidden well that Kitty had seen in her dream. What the subsequent excavation unearthed there – a gigantic Bronze Age heirloom, indeed made of solid gold – made them impossibly wealthy overnight. They asked Kitty to name the find; and they shared the wealth from its discovery with her. 'You were our muse,' Drox told Kitty as he and Max toasted her with champagne. 'The woman who inspired us to a great discovery, *a great deed.*'

Kitty knew better, but she kept silent. She knew that the true muse was not her, but *Katya.*

'I name the find, **The Goldheart**,' Kitty said and the three discoverers drank to it.

*K*itty quit tapping her cigarette on the tray table. There had been a special room for smokers, she remembered, on the *Fortes* oil rig. 'Self-discipline,' wasn't that her father's watchword? She slipped the Marlboro back into the pack, lifted her glass from the blue and white Pan Am coaster and drained her Bloody Mary. A stewardess took the glass and asked Kitty if she'd like another. 'Thank you, yes please,' Kitty said. She had been a stranger to First Class since she'd stopped flying with her father. She'd waited tables many a time as a runaway teenager, slept in cars, even slept on the street. Some are born to sweet delight, she thought. Not me. Some are born to endless night, more like. The stewardess handed her a refill. Kitty looked down into the cocktail glass, stirred the tomato juice and thought to herself: it's the color and consistency of clotting blood – I wonder what it's like to die?

A week before, Max had called her to say that The Goldheart had been insured at the Metropolitan Museum of Art in New York at twenty billion dollars – making it the most valuable archaeological artefact of all time – and making Kitty Maguire the fourth most wealthy woman in the world.

Now she was flying home (or at least to the sprawling Manhattan loft in the Garment District that Hart had just purchased) and Kitty thought she just might try to do some good in the world. She'd tried running away from home, getting pregnant at fourteen, disgracing her father, and giving her daughter one name to piss him off and another to please her mother: Boudica Valentina. She'd nurtured the fanciful thought that if she ever had a son, she would call him *William* after her father, to make up for it. Since Boudica's adoption she'd seen her daughter only twice.

Kitty looked down at her Bloody Mary, and a tear landed in it. She stirred the drink with the blue Pan Am straw, threw it down on her table and knocked the drink back. I really hit the spot, she told herself, the number one spot for the world's worst fucking mother.

Fuck it, she said to herself. Fuck it and fuck oil companies. Fuck trying to make money. Out loud she said, 'The whole world's in Auschwitz. It's where the big buck really stops.' But no one on the deck heard her. Insanely she wanted someone to hear, to look disdainfully and say, 'Young lady, you are disturbing other passengers. Will you kindly keep such dangerous thoughts to yourself.'

She imagined looking back at that person – it would be a man of course – and with her best madwoman look say with even greater determination, 'The whole world's in Auschwitz. It's where the buck really stops.'

*K*itty had brought a book with her. She had picked it up at a second-hand book shop in London because the cover caught her attention and reminded her of what she had just been through. It was a black and white photograph of towering, ominous clouds. It wasn't even in English, but she still bought it. The title read

> *Der Jüngste Tag: Ein Buch an die Menschheit, das von den kommenden Dingen spricht.*

Kitty had lived in Berlin, spoke German and read it adequately. The language in the book was convoluted. It was weird stuff, but Kitty had come of age in the seventies and she liked weird shit. Maybe it would give her some clue to the future. Switching on the reading light, Kitty opened the hardback near the beginning and removed her bookmark – a Polaroid of her estranged daughter at her tenth birthday party:

Boudica in a swimsuit – a Mexican beach at sunset – Kitty's mother Jane (image of an adoring grandmother) – a pair of Carmelite nuns (holding Scuba diving gear in child's size). With her hand, Boudica proudly strummed a guitar.

Kitty flipped over the Polaroid to reveal her father's handwriting

> Caba Teresa. September 28th 1988. Boudica's 10th.
> I hear congratulations are in order over the Goldheart. Not sure what you did exactly, but Hart says you played a crucial role. Here's Boudica – she's taking after you already. Hope London's not too cold. Dad.

Kitty wiped her tears. God help her if she is, she thought

6.2

— RETURNING TO FRIDAY, MARCH 13, 2015 —

10:45 p.m.

Schönefeld Airport, Neukölln District, Berlin, Germany

*P*olish captain Edith Stein checked for 'Travoltas' on the twin EPR gauges of the General Electric CFM56 *Evolution* turbofans and, seeing none, nodded to her co-pilot who opened the throttles. Stein released the ground brake and the last flight to London set off. The woman in seat 32A also had green eyes, but you wouldn't know it because she wore brown contact lenses as part of her disguise.

Ryanair flight 8545, out of Berlin's smaller airport, was to one of London's smaller airports, Stansted in Essex. Nobody who was anybody in espionage used Heathrow – not if they wanted to get into England undetected. She was travelling on a Swiss passport in the name of Aude Halpern. It was bumpy she thought. Yes, the north runway was in need of the refurbishment it was awaiting. As a pilot herself, like her aunt Valentina, KGB Captain Lara Starikova felt the engines pause slightly on the take-off roll.

Looking out the window at the aircraft's metal wing extending into the thin German night, Lara thought back to her meeting with her aunt earlier that day. As always when thinking of her aunt, famous for being the first woman in space, Lara felt a certain low-key tension in her heart. She loved her aunt – yes, she could say that clearly – but she was also intimidated by her. Mixed in with her love was the taint of resentment and fear. She remembered her aunt's curt official description of the mission: 'We have strong evidence MI6 will take the next step and kill Grinin. Go to London.

Protect him. Offer him a total amnesty to come home. Are you up to it?' Always the sting. Haven't I proven myself over and over again? Lara stopped herself. Old thoughts. No use going over them. Are you up to it . . . The family name, always the family name. As full throttle was engaged, Lara switched on her reading light and opened the hefty book on her lap: an English translation of Dostevsky's *The Idiot*. She'd read it twice in Russian, and was now making her second attempt to read it in English. Not because she found it difficult – but because she did not approve of Constance Garnett's translation. Mrs. Garnett, she told her literary friends, puts too much milk in Dostoyevsky's good black Russian tea. Lara was trying the David Magarshack translation.

Having just seen the photograph of Nastasia, the Prince describes his encounter with Rogozhin, the troubled young man who intends to marry Nastasia but goes on to murder her two weeks later. Lara glanced down at the page. Where was I? Ah, yes. 'What was your impression, Prince?' He's asking about Rogozhin. 'There was a good deal of passion in him, a sort of morbid passion.' Is that right? Morbid passion? Hard to capture the Russian sense. Doesn't he say the same thing about Nastasia? She skipped back to the point where the Prince first sees Natasia's photograph

> *The portrait was indeed of an extraordinarily beautiful woman ...*
> *photographed in a black silk dress of an extremely simple and*
> *elegant cut; her hair, which appeared to be a dark brown color,*
> *was done in a simple, homespun style ... her forehead was*
> *pensive; her expression was passionate and, as it were, haughty*

Not morbid passion – haughty passion. So many subtleties. Impossible to translate Russian passion. Can't even think of the Russian word now. Am I still a real Russian when I think in English? Nastasia going to her death, like cousin Kitty. An extraordinarily beautiful woman, like Kitty. What had Valentina said? 'If you have any trouble with Grinin, show him the photo.'

Lara lifted out the faded color photograph she was using as a bookmark. In the way that cousins sometimes look like sisters, the woman in the photograph clearly resembled Lara – although the woman was heavily pregnant. It was the last photograph of Kitty before she was murdered. December 1999 in front of the singing fountains of Peterhof Palace, St. Petersburg, taken by none other than Grigori Grinin. Lara remembered it: she had been there too, aged fourteen, with her aunt Valentina. 'You look so like her now,' Valentina had said. 'He has a strong bond with the Starikova family. Use his memory of Kitty to bring him back home.'

Being a Starikova was why Lara had been chosen for the mission thirty-six hours before. Her Sergeant was already in London with the hardware they would be deploying.

As the Boeing 737-800 ascended into the German cloud, it rocked and Lara slipped the last photograph of Kitty into the back cover

*N*early sat at a cafe table in the late night Foxes book store. Blanka had long gone and Nearby's CIA-Blue hadn't rung. All was quiet. She'd left home in a hurry, without her usual book and been out all day. Sometimes it was hard to keep up. On Wednesday Blanka had gotten MI6 to accept Grinin making a vaccine for Metapox. Now, she thought, two days later and we're trying to stop the bloody KGB from kidnapping him back. Oh, there I go swearing... Nearby drained her organic apple juice and looked at the books on her table. Café Fox had classic books on their tables and she picked one up, Everyman's Library edition of Sheridan's plays and opened it at *The School For Scandal*. It had, 'Dramatis Personae as originally acted at Drury Lane Theatre in 1777' and a prologue, 'Written by Mr. Garrick.' Nearby's great-grandmother had lived at number 3 Garrick Street, W.C.2. She remembered sitting on her father's lap and him telling her how as a boy he would break up fruit boxes from the old Covent Garden fruit and vegetable market to fuel his grandmother's kitchen range. The timer on her iPhone beeped. The Paris flight had landed. Passengers would arrive on two shuttles, the first due in thirty minutes.

In the science fiction book aisle Nearby found the book she was looking for, *Fahrenheit 451*. She'd seen an old analog film version of the Truffaut movie the month before at The Gate in Notting Hill and she loved the stars Oskar Werner and Julie Christie. She remembered seeing the credit, 'Based on the novel by Ray Bradbury.' She'd looked him up. Loved science fiction as a kid but the libraries didn't stock 'those' kind of novels. Not 'literary'. Then came the Nazi book burnings, Stalin's Great Purge, the communist witch hunts in America. They gave him a profound contempt for government overreach. So he wrote *Fahrenheit 451* about a society where Truth is outlawed and firemen burn books. Nearby thought about her own work as a Crown Servant for the British Government, at *Wonderland*. She looked down at her feet and noticed the gold and red Persian rug on the floor of the aisle. Sweeping things under the carpet is the least of it, she reflected.

To Nearby, the gagging of History, the destruction of art and religious artefacts and the burning of books was all of one kind. One of *her* earliest memories was of crying when she heard that the Taliban in Afghanistan had blown-up the biggest Buddha in the world.

She paid for *Fahrenheit 451*, dropped it into her bag, headed for the concourse and gave her full attention to the schedule of passengers on the remaining flights. She had photographs of Lara Starikova and the usual suspects the KGB might send and she had memorized them all (they were taught to do that in spy school). After

Paris there was only one more flight, from Berlin Schönefeld. Those passengers weren't due until 2 a.m. so it was going to be a long night.

*T*he passengers from the second Paris shuttle trooped out from platform 7 in pairs, singles and a few family groups and made their way to other trains, the subway, buses or taxis, or were met by friends. Nearby didn't see any KGB agents among them. When the passengers had gone, it left only four armed Met police on the concourse, so she headed past the public sculpture again for the stairs up to Foxes. As she passed the bronze she noticed the title: *Für Das Kind*. Her German was MI6-taught but she knew what it meant: For the child. Someone had put white roses at the children's feet. Perhaps a gesture of solidarity. Only now refugees were trying to escape *into* Europe, rather than *out of it*. She shivered in the cold and hurried up the steps.

At Café Fox she ordered a hot chocolate and a Latte (before they washed out the machines), a cranberry flapjack and an 'OMG' slice. Blanka had given her a packet of Lindors, but she didn't fancy chocolates. Chocolate was really bad for Blanka, but no one dared stop her. Sokol was the only one who even dared to mention it. Nearby loved Blanka but it was hard to live up to the standards of the most highly regarded Intelligence agent in the world whose worst sin was chocolate.

There were rumours about the hits Blanka did. Only rumours. But there were never any *bodies*. Maybe Blanka had more terrifying secrets than *chocolate addiction*. Anyway she was saving the Lindors in case she ended up at 5 a.m.-God-knows-where-following -a-target. It would be so much easier if Operation Tea Leaf wasn't being hidden from *everybody*. MI6, MI5, Special Branch, the Met police, British Transport police; MI4! The barista placed her latte on the tray and took her payment in cash. He smiled at Nearby and Nearby smiled back. Café Fox was empty now except for her and the barista. What about the Foxes staff? What if they grew suspicious? For some reason this made her giggle and the barista winked at her. Nearby, blushing, carried her tray to a different table by the window (also with a commanding view of platform 7). Why couldn't everyone be on the same side? she thought. She gulped back some of her latte and started on the 'OMG' slice. She chewed it slowly and gratefully.

She checked the time (another hour before the Berlin passengers), sipped her hot chocolate, contemplated the dark, creamy liquid and thought, why didn't I get two coffees? I'm not in a chocolate mood. She imagined Julie Christie, how she loved her other films. Pete says I look like her. When she was in her heyday. But really she looks more like Kitty. Or did Kitty look more like her? If two people look exactly like each other, who looks like who? Felicity and me. And what about twins? Oh, I'm getting muddled. Can't think straight.

Some one had left a book open on the table across from her. A reproduction of a first edition. She chuckled, reached for it and opened the front piece. It read

'Ulysses' by James Joyce. Shakespeare and Company, Paris

She thought of the illustration of the Ha'penny Bridge in Dublin on the cover of her copy, the River Liffey back home. She saw herself there with her own mother, and thought about Blanka and Kitty. *Kitty.* She really felt she knew her. Just then the book's most famous sentence leapt into her head

— History, Stephen said, is a nightmare from which I am trying to awake

Kitty's very pretty, thought Nearby. Joyce's daughter was pretty too. A dancer. Lucia: that'd been her name. Dated Samuel Beckett. Counselled by the great Carl Jung. Zürich, diagnosis schizophrenia. English mental hospital, thirty five years.

Her father's muse. Forgotten. *Written out of history*. Nearby remembered

Lucia!

Kitty had gone off in search of *Lucia!* A different Lucia

Lucia of Fatima. The shepherd girl.
And Kitty had been written out of history too

A tear of indignation welled up and ran down Nearby's cheek. Shut up, stop crying, she told herself. But her mind wouldn't quiet down. Hitler said Genghis Khan was only remembered as the founder of the world's greatest empire. What about the rest of the world? The people who weren't the masters of war or words? If only Dylan'd been right when he wrote *Masters of War*. But size does matter. What kinda history do ordinary people get – *zip, nada, nothing.*

The tear landed on the title. Nearby stared at the letter 'Y' through the glistening curve her eye had created. The clever Greek, the one who was trying to get home. Mr. James Joyce, you bloody Irish poet. What were you trying to do? Two men are lost, you get Leopold home, drunk though he may be. But Stephen continues to wander. We know, we feel, he'll eventually write the novel we're reading. He'll escape the nightmare of history the only way he can – by writing his own history. The true history of that bloody, priest-ridden race. His Ireland.

That's it! Nearby thought. She almost shouted *Eureka*. The central event of *Ulysses* was the novel's own creation. Perhaps the central event of History too was writing it down. As it was written, so shall it be. The biggest gun and the biggest book and the biggest movie: those are the people who create History, and they create the future too. Hitler and Stalin and Democracy tell us what to do; Homer, Shakespeare and Cookies tell us what to see significance in. She took a tissue from her bag and dabbed the corner of her eye. You stupid Irish tart, who cries over something like that?

Someone, some *ordinary* person, should dig the *corpus historiarum* up, she thought. Exhume the effing facts, suck the putrid core from the marrow, test its mitochondrial DNA – like the bones of King Dickie the Third carried forth from under a Leicester car park into the penetrating light of day; write everything down, even the footnotes however bad they smell; eyeball History, shout, '*imposter!*' to its face – and be done with it.

At that moment the station was empty, the lights were low, and in the reflection of the window glass, she could see the faint outline of her face against the strangely fluid darkness.

Saturday. 00:20 a.m.
London Stansted Airport, Bishops Stortford, Essex, UK

As the 737 descended the final hundred feet on to the east runway, Lara's reading light was out but she had the book open in her lap. She still held the last photograph of Kitty. Valentina had been very close to Kitty's late mother, Jane. They had been together, at Kitty's side, when she had given birth to Blanka in 1978.

Lara and Blanka had met half a dozen times. Unknown to both Russian and Western Intelligence they exchanged birthday and Christmas cards. Blanka's such a Libran, reflected Lara as the wheels hit the tarmac, she sends me little gifts. But Kitty's a Mars sign like me. I'm Aries, she was a Scorpio. Did Kitty's nickname, 'J.F.K.' reflect that?
'Every American knows where they were when J.F.K. was assassinated,' Valentina had told her. 'And Cousin Kitty *was being born*.' One soul takes off, another lands, thought Lara, as Captain Stein sent the EPR gauges spinning by engaging the thrust reversers on the engines. 'J.F.K. spelt trouble!' Valentina had often said.

Lara looked out at the green grass of England flying past the airplane window, gray in the airport night. As the aircraft braked to a mere fifteen knots and turned onto its taxiway, Lara contemplated Kitty's big green eyes, so like her own under their brown contacts.

Valentina had summed Kitty up like this: she was a girl who never had to look for trouble, because trouble came looking for her.

*T*he shuttle train was held up two hours with a signalling fault. It was the early hours before dawn on Saturday when Lara put her ticket into the automatic barrier at Liverpool Street Station and stepped from platform 7 onto the concourse, empty except for the four Met police talking to a group of hungover girls who'd been clubbing in the West End. The police glanced at Lara and the other exhausted passengers arriving from Stansted and returned to their conversation. Lara had been to London this way before and headed straight for the subway, the tube.

As she approached the entrance, the six-foot-high bronze sculpture stopped her in her tracks. The girl of eight stood determinedly beside an old fashioned trunk, her younger brother sat dejected on the floor, his hands on the legs of his shorts, the white roses at their feet. Very Narnia-esque thought Lara. She'd just spent five hours in Berlin and the bronze brought a lump to her throat. She knew about the Kindertransport – a drop of goodness on the brink of an ocean of horror – she didn't know why but she'd always been interested.

She had read about the Flor Kent sculptures created to commemorate it. Originally a glass suitcase had contained the actual artefacts brought over to London by the Jewish children arriving by the transport before the invasion of Czechoslovakia and Poland. The first 196 Kindertransport children had been rescued from a burning Berlin orphanage, set on fire during the infamous *Kristallnacht*, Crystal Night or Night of Broken Glass. The symbolic beginning of *The Holocaust*.

Lara felt physically sick. Why hadn't she eaten in Berlin?

The sculpture could not but evoke Katya and Elsa – her other two aunts – born a decade before her father Ivan, and Valentina. The children of the Kindertransport had escaped murder and worse at Auschwitz, even though her father's sisters had not been so fortunate.

More than ten thousand were saved by the Kindertransport in the last minute of the eleventh hour before World War Two. If all the parents had seen what was coming, reasoned Lara, maybe millions would have been sent… Without looking, she felt the eyes of a Met officer on her back. She hurried away with her cabin bag and stumbled slightly on the steps down to the Central line and her rendez-vous with her KGB Sergeant at 07:30 hours. With luck she might get two hours sleep.

From her vantage point at Café Fox, Nearby was perfectly sure of her target. She pressed a code button on the CIA-Blue and sent a 'target acquired' signal to the Blue control in Blanka's stable. Lara Starikova was well disguised but without a prosthetic face mask appliance she did not fool Nearby. She was an easier target to follow than Nearby had expected. As she changed to the south bound Victoria line at Oxford Circus, Nearby was already there. Standard tailing-from-in-front procedure. Although normally they'd be half a dozen agents 'tailing' one target, Nearby prided herself that she did it better than any other officer in the Russia Desk. She tailed Lara to her hotel then reported in to Blanka on the Blue and started the long wait to be relieved

9:25 a.m.
Victoria Embankment, S.W.1

*T*wo MI6 agents on assignment to OhZone pretended to take photos on the steps to River Heights, while MI6 and OhZone surveillance teams watched from different vantage points. One agent was a very tired Nearby.

She had not been relieved, but reassigned to pretend to take fashion photographs of her colleague, another glamorous young woman from the Russia Desk, Black British, born in Wales, and living with her grandmother in W.2 (*not* the Edgeware Road spy hostel). Everyone called her 'Paddington'.

Nearby and Paddington were there as a deterrent to the KGB. Yes, not even Vladimir Putin could have arranged what happened next. In order to battle cyber-terrorism, MI6 was recruiting sixteen-year-olds and the first (from Sheffield and already nicknamed 'Wednesday' after the soccer team) was starting after the weekend. They were *transgender*, so it was that a 'Sullivan, Gilbert and Son' truck bearing a Portacabin with Port-a-John, emblazoned with transgender restroom insignia, passed River Heights on its way from E.16 to MI6. 'It's the transgender restroom for Wednesday!' exclaimed Paddington. Nearby photographed it in front of Big Ben. 'It's in good time for Monday,' she laughed, 'I think I'll Tweet it.'

Comrade Putin had however arranged a band of young women, looking like a hungover hen party, who turned the corner, shouted un-ladylike remarks at the Port-a-John truck and shambled into Victoria Embankment obstructing traffic and completing the diversion.

*L*ara, now dressed in blue engineer's overalls, smiled to herself as she watched it all from a black BMW SUV (like so many others in the West End) sixty yards down the river. Mr Putin's former associates had kindly fitted the SUV with special mesh within the smoked glass to create an Archimedes cage impervious even to ℧Scanners.

Lara's Sergeant nodded to the driver and concluded his briefing on the status of the operation, while in the back an embassy technician applied the finishing touch to the prosthetic appliance over Lara's face. It transformed her Russian features to those of a younger Middle Eastern woman. The Russians watched Crusoe (in green water board overalls) hear about the transgender Port-a-John on his earpiece, laugh and walk up Richmond Terrace.
Lara wrapped a hijab over her face as the driver pulled out north, turned up Horse Guards Avenue, drove fifty yards back down Whitehall and into the other end of Richmond Terrace. They were

in time to see Crusoe, now at the rear of River Heights, step into the back of a water company truck, where he relieved Hans (a German agent waiting to be enrolled into OhZone) who sat slumped next to Farringdon at the bank of thirty monitors showing the outside and inside of River Heights. Five monitors were black.

Hans smiled. 'Lara Starikova is here, she dropped in via Berlin.'
Crusoe raised his eyebrows.
'We don't have the resources apparently –' started Hans.
'We *are* short staffed –'
'– to anticipate the KGB's moves, so the big plan is to stop them getting Grinin or his family out of the building.'
'If that's what they intend to do.'
'If that's what they intend to do. Anyway Grinin was up early as usual disabling the cameras and half the bugs.'
'Telephone engineer back in?' asked Farringdon.
'Yep,' replied Crusoe. 'Anything else?'
'They ate breakfast at 08:30 before he hacked the camera in there,' Farringdon continued, 'and Diana's just left for Sea Life with the kids.' Crusoe nodded and Farringdon yawned back: he wasn't going home. Hans offered around his packet of Marlboro White, 'Something for the weekend?'
Crusoe and Farringdon feigned smiles and took cigarettes.
'One smoke then I'm off for a wundersleep.'

Hans lit the cigarettes and Farringdon called on the Scanner. Sokol answered. 'We need the telephone engineer back,' Farringdon said.

Hans and Crusoe were suddenly glued to monitors: A woman, bearing an engineer's case, was accessing the rear entrance with the 'Trade' button. Hans zoomed the monitor into a frame of her overalls. The logo read, 'London Aquarium Maintenance'.
'Could be for Grinin. Have they been before?' asked Crusoe.

Farringdon ran back through the written log whilst telling Sokol, 'Aquarium maintenance is here, we think for him.'
'Of course it's for him,' said Sokol, 'He's got the biggest tank outside Sea Life. I'll get the telephone engineer on his way.'

*T*he private key elevator light lit Penthouse, the door opened and Lara stepped out into Grinin's plush hall.

She had not met the notoriously eccentric Chess Grand Master and Nobel Laureate since she was fifteen, but Grinin did not disappoint. He stood in front of her on a red, blue and gold Turkish carpet, wearing a Kashmir housecoat and matching slippers, and holding a children's balloon pump in his one hand.

He smiled (sympathetically Lara thought) but said nothing. Lara noticed the Royal Doulton toby jug of Queen Elizabeth the Second on the fine antique table beside him. As the elevator door closed, Grinin turned and walked into his enormous lounge, where Russian fine art jostled for space on the walls with originals by Man Ray and David Hockney, and the *1812 Overture* boomed from a vinyl record. Lara followed and was staggered that the aquarium she was supposedly there to service occupied a sixth of the room. The Grinins' long-legged Russian Nanny stood on a short ladder hanging up decorations and balloons for Emma and Olga's birthday party.
'I have to attend to the fish now!' Grinin shouted above the music to the Nanny. She nodded, finished hanging a banner reading

С днем рождения 3

and climbed down. The canons fired in the climax to the music, and Grinin grabbed the Nanny and waltzed her around the aquarium, grinning at Lara as they passed. As the drums rolled, he took a slip of paper from a pocket. 'Do the shopping now. These for the party, this from the post office.'

'*Khorosho*,' nodded the Nanny taking a pair of spectacles from her pocket and handing it to him. 'Madame says to wear your distance glasses.' The playing arm lifted from the record, Grinin flashed her a false smile and she headed for the elevator.

Lara looked at the view from the panoramic window. It took in a fine stretch of river from the London Eye to the Palace of Westminster. Lara noticed the bronze sculpture of Boudica on her chariot at the foot of Big Ben and thought of Blanka.

Grinin softly closed the door behind the Nanny. Putting on the glasses, he looked at Lara more intently. 'Somehow I don't think you know very much about aquaria. Come close so I can see you. Take that thing off, there's no camera in here.'

Lara tugged off the hijab, approached to a couple of feet and politely held out her left hand to shake his.

Grinin took a spray bottle of DNA-denaturing solvent and a pack of forensic wipes from his pocket. 'I like to cover all the traces,' he said. 'Agents of all sorts come and go as they like here, water people, telephone people...'

'Butchers, bakers and candle-stick makers,' suggested Lara and held out her hands for him to spray and wipe down.

'Your English is impeccable,' he said as he kissed her on both cheeks, Russian style.

'It helps,' said Lara gesturing to the walls.

'I leave some bugs working so they think they have me under surveillance,' Grinin responded, 'but I swept in here this morning. I remember you having green eyes.' Lara smiled at his humour.

'You have one thing and one thing alone of interest to me, Captain.'

'And what is that, Major?'

Grinin ran his hand along the aquarium glass and stared at a group of red and white fish. 'A little bird tells me that the little girl I taught to play chess –'

'Has grown into a big girl?'

Grinin ushered Lara into one of a pair of antique armchairs arranged with a chess table between them, with pieces in three colors: white, red and black.

'Has kept up her study of the game, unlike your older cousin, who is a very disappointing and erratic chess player.'

'And Sokol visited you yesterday,' Lara said. 'Since you're both defectors, it must have reminded you of the old days.'

'Yes. She said she might deign to play if I agree to have someone in the flat around the clock. The group at the British Library are my only consolation.' He laid out the white pieces on one side of the chess table.

'You have black as well as red.'

'Three is a key number. Rule of three. Three colors of quarks. Three states of matter.'

'Three sides all wanting you. The British Prime Minister is so worried about you, he's sending MI5 to guard you as well.'

Grinin shrugged. 'The more the merrier.'

'Three's a crowd?'

'And what are you, *Charlie's Angels*? OhZone are moving us to Dublin. President Obama arranged it. Are the Irish much in the way of chess, do you think?'

'I've never been there.'

Lara picked up the black king. 'You will never make the vaccine there. Because OhZone cannot protect you – from *this*.'

Grinin scrutinised the black king.

'Four of your weapons were sold off,' she reminded him.

Grinin took the black king from Lara's fingers. 'But not to *here*.'

'No, not to *there*. But it's only a matter of time. *We* can protect you. Complete pardon, your old life, Petersburg suburb. Freedom for

Diana and the children to come and go as they please.'

'But no international travel for me?'

'We want to protect you.'

Have me on hand to get Dr Carlos out of trouble, more like, he thought. 'It's touching everyone is so concerned for my welfare,' he said. 'But I'm tired of hiding. Hiding from others, hiding from myself. I'm planning a road trip.'

'What?'

'To see the western edge of Europe. I'll go alone, on Wednesday. Monday I'm at the BBC, Tuesday is our wedding anniversary, five years.'

'Congratulations.'

'Thank you.' Grinin had finished lining up the white pieces and had both the black and red kings in his hand.

'Which color?'

Lara took the last photograph of Kitty from the metal case. 'The color of valour,' she said as she handed it to Grinin. Grinin sighed and put the two kings back on the table. 'I was so hoping you wanted to play chess. Instead, you want to play this game.' He stared at the photo. 'A game of tears, why do you want to play it?'

'I saw you take the picture. You saved her life.'

'It was the picture of a dead woman. I think I knew it at the time.'

'You saved Kitty.'

Grinin scoffed. 'For a short while.'

'She was murdered by the people who want to murder you now.'

Grinin shook his bear-like head. 'So you are showing a picture of a dead woman, to a dead man? What kind of game is that?'

'An end game?'

'So we're back to chess? And Valentina wants to put Kitty on the board. What kind of piece shall we make her? She played with the bishops, many bishops... the German one in particular.'

Lara was out of her depth, tiredness was hitting, her eyes glazing over.

'A queen? A knight?' Grinin continued, 'The poor girl should have stayed a pawn.'

'What about Diana? Emma, Olga?'

'They do not belong on the board. And neither does Kitty.' Grinin smiled and rubbed his hand on the side of his aquarium, drawing several fish towards him. Lara watched him carefully.

'I'm not certain, but I think the dead don't stay in the game,' he said, watching the fish. 'Do you know one of the strategies used in an end game?'

Lara felt herself floundering, 'What do you mean?'

'Most of the advice is about how to use pawns, but one thing you can also do is surprise the opponent by activating your king. Make the king an attack piece.'

Lara saw an opportunity and brought out a 5 kilo Russian diplomatic pouch from the case, broke the seals and placed a pair of Gyurza 9mm pistols on the chess table. 'If you are going to attack,' she said, 'Here's something you can attack with.'

Grinin picked up one of the pistols and studied it as if it were some curious artefact from a Bronze Age civilization. 'It would make a *strange chess piece indeed*. Not particularly elegant. Tell Valentina she shouldn't send me *such toys*, I wouldn't use them that way. I'd use them *backwards*, a bullet through my head is a great temptation. You see I'm not really trying to attack – I'm trying to *escape*. I'm going to declare '*stalemate*' and leave the board. The fox is going to lead the hounds *away from his den*.'

Lara felt the conversation getting seriously out of her control, if it ever had been in her control. Kitty's son, she suddenly thought! 'You talk about Kitty being a dead woman but you saved her long enough,' Lara announced, 'For her to have a son! Will. You did save Will's life.'

Grinin handed Lara the photo of Kitty, forcing her to accept it. 'That's true and I suppose he must be about fifteen now. The dead continue in the living. But not quite. I've been thinking lately about a poem by an English poet, Tennyson. It's about Ulysses in his old age. An *idle king*, he calls him. Have you read it?'

Numb, Lara could only shake her head. 'What are you going to do?' She hated herself for sounding so meek, like a schoolgirl trying to question an overpowering teacher.

'I don't see the harm. While the hounds are busy dissecting my situation, while they are barking, I shall simply leave. I will drive to Ireland!'

'Drive? You don't drive!' Lara felt the air empty out of her lungs.

'I have a licence. I have just booked a rental car A fine red Range Rover. An ocean voyage, sea air! I shall see the Emerald Isle! Explore Galway, Limerick, the West Coast.'

'The West Coast? Away from your family? You'll drive to your death, you must know that?'

'Ah, but if you're *going that way...* what does Ulysses say to his men? "Come, my friends, / Tis not too late to seek a newer world." '

'I'm here to protect you. If you're on your own, they will get to you and finish you off.'

'*Finish me off*?! Lara listen! These are the wonderful last words in the poem – when Ulysses admits he has been, "made weak by time and fate" but that he's still, "strong in will / To strive, to seek, to find, and not to yield." '

Lara gaped at Grinin – speechless – while he playfully fed fish-treats to his beloved fish. Finally he turned to her. 'Don't you see? Not to yield, *not to go gently.* That's the only *end game* I can live with' ʊ

The Secret Carpet

Caesar:
Who is it in the press that calls on me?
I hear a tongue shriller than all the music
Cry 'Caesar!' Speak, Caesar is turn'd to hear.

Soothsayer:
Beware the ides of March.

WILLIAM SHAKESPEARE - JULIUS CAESAR

Felicity's house, Jermyn Grove, Balham, S.W.12

*H*er head submerged under the deep bathwater in her vintage claw leg high-sided enamelled bath, Felicity Robinson opened her eyes at exactly 11.14 a.m. and looked up at her ornate Victorian ceiling. When she raised her head, she let out an enormous breath, felt the bath water run from her long brown hair, and filled her lungs with oxygen. She loved fire and heat – and oxygen fed the fires – that's why she'd wanted to be an OhZone.

Johnny Depp had an identical tub, the man in Crystal Palace Vintage Houseware had told her. Around its edge and on the windowsill behind her head were a hundred twinkling tea lights, each in its own little glass. She looked sideways at her iPhone [the same model and gold color as Nearby's] set on a marble pedestal beside her. She liked to race the timer on it. The clock turned 11:15, its alarm beeped, and her left arm reached out to dismiss it. The tattoo on her arm glistened under the drops of bathwater. Genghis glared and the small black swastika shone, but there were also tell-tale signs of other tattoos on her body, expensively removed by laser surgery. She turned on the tap, let steaming hot water tumble into the tub and purred – she was the Cheshire cat.

She didn't like the name Wonderland, she only said it sometimes to bait C. Or *Alice*. She didn't care for dreams: nonsense and imagination, fanciful stuff her new husband Jude liked. Jude would be arriving at the Russia Desk shortly for his sixteen hour back-to-back shifts. He had been good company Thursday night at their dinner party for friends; but he, like them, was another stranger to her. Felicity looked over the enamel side of the tub at the black and white chequered floor. She liked sensible, solid, tangible things. She had had a wood floor laid throughout the house, but now they could afford hardwood. She could pay for it out of the extra salary she would get for the black hit, but she didn't want to. Let Jude pay for it, she thought. Like the generous 'allowances' for foreign postings, a blue-slip hit paid generously and it was tax-free. It stood to reason that a Black Slip hit must pay even more. Crown Servant, C's mistress, Grade 4, OhZone and now a Black Slip. She was doing well, her financial plans were on track. Soon she could start to build her facility. And a dame-hood would be nice too.

Her bathroom was immaculate like a virgin, never spoiled by use. She liked it that way. She poured herself more Earl Grey tea from a Victorian silver teapot and sipped it gratefully. As she leant back against the end of the bath, the main tattoo that hadn't been removed was displayed – stretched not over one C-cup breast but over two – a tattooed map of the world. And the map concerned made it a truly unique breast decoration. A 1325 A.D. map, of the world as conquered by Genghis Khan. She lifted her foot from the water, with perfectly aligned and polished crimson painted toe-nails and switched off the hot tap with her big toe. She submerged herself again. The tattooed breasts sank into the steam and disap-peared under the water. But her big nipples remained prominent above the surface. She looked down at them: like submarine conning towers, she thought, twin towers, alert to all comers.

*F*elicity hadn't stayed the night at C's, she'd left after a cup of Earl Grey tea, and told him to pick her up at one o'clock for the ribbon cutting ceremony. She had recently become the youngest trustee and it was her job to cut the ribbon and open the fete. Although the Society did not use the Bethlem site as an orphan-age any more, it was the largest charity in London pushing for a new generation of children's institutions. Felicity had made it a special project of hers to raise new funds for their new-build 21st century orphanage of the future. Blanka has her animals, she thought, and I have my orphans.

Shortly after one o'clock, Felicity sat on the pillion of C's silver BMW K1600 motorcycle as they rode past Chestnut Picture Gallery. The gallery was close to her Victorian house although, much to her annoyance, her house was on the wrong side of London's A24 trunk road. Now that she had Jude's salary as well as her own to play with she could move, if she wanted to. But she didn't and she continued to smile her big smile not because of the picture gallery but despite it. The snow had melted, the fog had lifted and the weak sun (so foreign to March in north-western Europe) struggled to shine on the suburb immortalized at the end of World War Two as *Bal-Ham, Gateway to the South.*

Felicity's liking for Balham had more to do with where they were headed – the site of the old Bethlem Orphanage. The number of young orphans [looked-after-children, the government now termed them] had increased in England by over twenty per cent in the last ten years. Felicity's interest lay with the three quarters of them who were white, some of whom were helped by the S.W.12 headquarters of the London Christian Orphans Society.

C turned a couple of corners into Emmanuel Park and slowed the motorcycle outside a large Victorian building colorfully bedecked for a Saturday afternoon carnival. He pulled in through the ornate gates and under the iron Victorian sign, 'Orphanage.' As he pulled to a stop in the staff car park, Felicity hopped off. She removed her helmet as the elderly president of the Society marched out. The woman greeted Felicity warmly but squinted at C, unable to make him out in his motorcycle gear. C was left to amuse himself while the lady president showed Felicity into the building. The fair was crowded with local families coming along to enjoy the fun fair and games, and would-be benefactors who believed that a new generation of institutional care stood a better chance of imparting 'suitable values' than fostering.

As Felicity cut the ribbon on the three-legged race event that opened the sports, she was smiling her big smile. This was a new beginning, people were taking her seriously, taking her ideas seriously; maybe not C and Bio, but others were.

★

*L*ater Felicity, sporting a huge bunch of helium-filled balloons in all the colors of the rainbow, walked through the crowd. Whenever she passed a child or a teenager she handed them a colored balloon. As each of them took a balloon she carefully looked them in the eyes. Other trustees acknowledged her proudly. 'That's what we need,' the president said to her husband, 'more fresh blood like Robinson. And she's an orphan herself.' 'I see,' he said. 'Is that her husband running the bagatelle?' 'No, he has to work,' the president answered. 'That's her uncle.'

Felicity felt vindicated at the respect that was shown to her. She'd show C and Bio and the other doubters at The Office. She went from one stall to another spending money at each and chatting amiably to the stallholders. At the American Candy Stall she chose two paper bagful's of candy and put them away carefully in her bag. Eventually she bought four sticks of pink candyfloss from the candyfloss stall. Two were for her favourite boys, the brothers Jimmy and Brian. She looked for them among the crowd. She'd have liked to have kept the other two candyfloss for two other children, but she knew the candy wouldn't keep.

As Felicity walked through some trees to another part of the grounds, she looked some more for Jimmy and Brian. She still didn't see them so she tried whistling the opening bars from the whistle in the film, *Twisted Nerve*. That particular whistle would only attract Jimmy (the older and bolder brother). Sometimes it worked and sometimes it didn't. She stopped whistling and listened for an answer. There it was, an answering whistle, the theme from *The Great Escape*. From behind a tree a tall boy of ten came running up to her.
'Hello Jimmy,' she said, handing him the first candyfloss. 'Where's Brian?'
'He's about somewhere, Miss.'
Felicity handed him the second candyfloss. 'For Brian. And here's some spending money for you both,' she smiled, handing him two ten-pound notes. 'You remember about tomorrow? What we planned?'
'Oh yes, Miss.'
'OK, enjoy yourself.'

She went to the badge-making stall and ordered two badges. C watched from the stall next door where he was running the Bagatelle. He didn't have any customers. As the badges were being stamped out, she crossed to C and handed him the third candy-floss, biting into the last one herself.

'How much longer do I have to mind this stall,' asked C.

'Man up,' answered Felicity, 'do your bit for society.'

C frowned at her and she returned to collect her badges. The badge woman handed them over. They read

Emma and Olga

7.2

Sunday, March 15. 7:55 a.m.
River Heights, Victoria Embankment, S.W.1

*A*s one-armed Grigori Grinin stepped out of the rotating door of River Heights he tried valiantly not to look old. There was a spring in his step as he descended the wide steps on his journey to confession at the Russian Orthodox cathedral. But he *was* old. Almost of another age, more like Rasputin or Sherlock Holmes, than a 21st century man. And like a pagan ritual in which a god is paraded through the streets, a procession formed behind him. It began with his wife, Diana. Then the Russian Nanny leading Emma in one hand and Olga (clutching her birthday-present toy tiger) in the other. The MI5 Woman from the newly-arrived MI5 protection team pushed the empty double buggy. She might as well do something useful, Grinin had said. The Special Branch officer standing outside the apartments then fell in with the procession as it turned right and walked up Victoria Embankment towards Big Ben. Lastly, from their position near Boudica's Chariot statue, came a second MI5 agent and Paddington.

The day before, Special Branch had announced to Grinin that he was no longer allowed, for security reasons, to pass Buckingham Palace, where the Queen was currently closeted. He had simply laughed. The officer had called in his superior, the Superintendent who had painstakingly explained that it was nothing personal about Major Grinin but the reassessment of two security zones: the Royal family, and the Grinin family. Grinin had said he was terribly sorry and it was nothing personal against Special Branch or the Saxe-Coburgs but he was sticking to his traditional Sunday route. 'How would you stop me,' he said. 'Shoot me?' In the end a compromise was reached: he had to write down his route for them and agree to be driven half the way. 'It will save on the taxi fare,' Diana had said, 'and there are nine of us now counting all the security escorts.'

✦

Grinin and his procession stopped at the west end of Westminster Bridge underneath Big Ben and outside the British Houses of Parliament. He called over the Special Branch officer, Andrew Gabor, British by birth but of Hungarian origin.
'Officer Gabor. I would like you to confirm something to my children.'
'To Emma and Olga sir?
Emma and Olga let go of the Nanny's hands and trotted closer.
'Yes, it's their birthday today.'
'Yes indeed, Sir. I'm looking forward to their party.'
'Are you coming to our party?' asked Olga
'Yes, I am,' said Gabor.
'See!' whispered Olga to Emma.

'And may I take this opportunity to say to both of you, *many happy returns*,' said Gabor.
'Now, will you inform my daughters of their nationality?'

Gabor squatted down and Emma took his hand. Olga stuck her tongue out at Emma, moved her now ever-present tiger to her left hand, and took Gabor's other hand.
'You are both British citizens because you were born here in London – in fact on the seventh floor of the hospital you can see across the river.'
'See, we *are* British,' said Olga to Emma.
'And Russian,' said Emma.
'We were born *here*.'
'I was born in the water pool, you weren't.'
'Well, I was born in London all the same.'
'Girls,' Grinin announced impatiently, 'I have a story for you. Do I have your attention?'
The twins stopped squabbling and in a comic fashion stood at attention before their imposing father. Diana couldn't help but smile.

'Many years ago when this country was at war with Hitler –'
'Who's he?' asked Emma in a cheeky voice.
'The Leader of Nazi Germany, they overran the whole of Europe.'
'Even Moscow?' asked Emma
'They tried to.'
'And London?' asked Olga
'They dropped many bombs. The House of Commons in here was *blown up*.' Grinin raised his arm, making a loud explosion sound, and the girls jumped. Hitler silenced all the bells in Europe, except this one.'
Grinin pointed to the Big Ben bell tower above and the twins followed his gaze. 'The Nazis stole the church bells from the occupied countries of Europe and turned them into guns.'
'Guns are bad,' said Olga, quietly.

Grinin looked down at his tiny daughter through his bushy beard and nodded, solemnly.

'In this Island, where the British struggled on alone –'

'We're British,' said Olga.

'– The British silenced their own church bells to stop the Nazis navigating by them.

'What's navi-gate-ing?' said Emma cheekily.

'It's finding your way,' said Diana

Emma turned to her sister and pointed west, 'It's walking into something you can't see, like us going to the cathedral.'

'We can't see it in front of us…' said Olga.

'Yes,' said Diana.

'To continue with my story. One summer day in 1941, Hitler invaded Russia, and Russia became the ally of Britain.'

'Alli-what?' said the cheeky voice. Her sister giggled.

'The Americans became allies as well and Hitler started slowly losing the War. The threat of invasion passed and the church bells of England rang out again, from Easter Sunday 1943.' Grinin looked at his watch, then nodded to Diana as a signal for her to hold the hands of the children.

A cacophony of sound started as the bells of Big Ben struck above them – its famous sixteen note signature theme for the hour. Startled, the twins looked up at their father, who was laughing, and they started laughing too. Big Ben went on to strike eight deep notes for the hour of eight o'clock.

'Such a big noise!' the twins said together.

*O*nce the bells had stopped, the procession turned into St James Park, participated in the ritual feeding of the ducks on the pond and then walked over the footbridge to The Mall. Grinin wanted photographs taken with Buckingham Palace in the background.

As the procession approached it down The Mall, Grinin decided it was the best view. Because of the security risk, two London bobbies and two armed Met police had now joined them.

The MI6 agents kept their distance as C had instructed. Blanka had stationed Sokol, still nominally a Russian Orthodox, inside the cathedral. Blanka, the only other OhZone in place, was in the sky a thousand feet above the cathedral in the new H175 high-speed helicopter. Nearby had the day off and had volunteered to do some gardening in Blanka's back yard (as she called it in American) while listening on the CIA-Blue.

Near the Cathedral, behind the trees, Felicity agent ℧7 was studying the twins' photograph, not because she didn't know what they looked like, but because she was fascinated by their combination of fair hair and brown eyes. No one detected her.

As the Grinin family lined up for the photographs, Emma spied a scarlet-colored Royal Mail post box and remembered excitedly that they had postcards to mail to Diana's father in Moscow (thanking him for their birthday presents). The Nanny's suggestion that the postcards could wait was met with suitable scorn.

'I'm going to post mine *now*,' said Emma. 'To Moscow.'

Olga pulled away from the Nanny, and ran to her father who was holding her toy tiger. With her tiny hands Olga took the tiger gently from her father's huge hand and said, 'Father, we want to post our cards to Grandfather.'

While Diana, the Nanny, officer Gabor, the MI5 officers and the police all watched the birdie, Grinin nipped to the post box with his daughters. Olga swung on his one arm, gripping her tiger in one hand and the postcard in the other, while Emma followed closely behind carrying hers. As Paddington later reported, it only took a moment. Two postcards and an old-fashioned blue airmail letter [to an address in Fiji] disappeared into the scarlet post box

9:30 a.m.
Russian Orthodox Cathedral, Knightsbridge, S.W.7

Sokol Camarovski, agent Ʊ5, believed that actions spoke louder than words, but as she sat in the cathedral at 67 Ennismore Gardens, S.W.7 watching Grigori Grinin kneel down in line to await the Eucharist, she had more in common with him than she realized. Not only had they both defected from the KGB, sharing a love both of music and their homeland, but they both also liked Oscar Wilde's *Ballad of Reading Gaol*. Sokol liked it because it was close, morbid and nihilistic. Grinin had come across it while he studied for his doctorate at Cambridge. That day, as he knelt, certain parts of Wilde's poem came to mind as he glanced up at the cathedral window high above him

> *I never saw a man who looked*
> *With such a wistful eye*
> *Upon that little tent of blue*
> *Which prisoners call the sky . . .*

There it was, he told himself as he looked up, 'that little tent of blue'. The hint of sky high above the cathedral ceiling only confirmed to him that he was a prisoner. There was no escape from his fate. As the chalice came slowly, inexorably closer, his eyes took in the immensity of the Cathedral. A grand structure, filled with icons, images both of hope and suffering. Yet, for him, more than anything else, it was the suffering of Christ that he felt, His suffering on the night of the last supper

> *and when he had given thanks, he broke it, and said, 'This is*
> *my body which is for you. Do this in remembrance of me.'*

When I am gone, what will people remember me for? he thought to himself. Metapox? I hope that's not all. Chess is better. For helping unearth the real Fatima Secret, better still. In that moment of waiting, certain of his own imminent death, Grinin thought about the deaths that had marked out the Starikova family – the death of the twins, so young, after unspeakable torture in the hands of Dr Mengele. And he included Kitty among the family's dead. Why else had Valentina urged Lara to show him the photo he had taken of her? To remember her as part of a family he had loved. To keep tears from his eyes, Grinin glanced furtively, angrily, around the cathedral. These images of Christ and His mother, His family. To remind us of His death. His suffering, our continued suffering. But His sacrifice meant there was an end to suffering… didn't it? Suddenly more lines from Wilde's poem echoed in his mind

> *He did not wear his scarlet coat,*
> *For blood and wine are red,*
> *And blood and wine were on his hands*
> *When they found him with the dead*

He smiled grimly. But I have only one hand now. Not one foot but one hand in the grave. Because of what I did, what I created with those hands. The Metapox. The Law of Karma has punished me, and justly so. The Lord giveth, and the Lord taketh away.

> *And bound with bars lest Christ should see*
> *How men their brothers maim*

Is Christ pleased by how I have been maimed? No, none of this pleases Him. And to think I fled Russia, my home, and thought I could escape. Did Kitty think she could escape? When I brought the icon to her, *The Magdalene?*

Did she see hope in it, or only more suffering? She saw purpose in it, something that brought her close to the Fatima Secret. But The

Magdalene led her to her death. I didn't save her, I condemned her. Another prisoner. Another nightmare. Another execution. That is what images do to us. Thank God, thought Grinin, that The Magdalene was so carefully locked away. And maybe, after all, it was a good thing that so very few people knew the real Secret: one or two old cardinals in Vatican Intelligence, maybe the Mother Superior of Lucia's convent, Kitty herself... and the one she shared it with... I told her to keep it in her heart and just go on home to New York City. 'Grigori.' He felt his wife gently nudge him. 'He is here. Have you forgotten the Eucharist?'

After he received the Eucharist from Father Deiniol, Diana helped her husband up and walked outside into the sunshine with him, followed by the children and the Nanny. At the door, uniformed police accompanied Major Grinin as the press appeared, the paparazzi, to take more photographs. The children were corralled next to their parents and the Nanny was alone.

★

*F*elicity had arranged show time for the moment when Grinin walked from the Cathedral followed by Sokol.

Prosthetics John let off thunder flashes in the back of a van, first sounding like gun shots then (on reflection) like a car back-firing, as ten-year-old Brian fell and cut his knee in front of Paddington. Sokol and the MI5 Woman leapt in front of Grinin, drawing their pistols and giving away their cover. While Paddington and the other officers were distracted by Brian, Felicity whistled her call for his brother Jimmy to act. Hearing his cue, Jimmy ran in with three helium balloons from the orphans' fair (a red one, a white one and a blue one) and handed them to Emma and Olga. As they clutched the balloons excitedly and fought over the third, the wind blew their blonde hair in their eyes and over their faces and the press photographers couldn't get their shots. The Nanny produced a hairbrush from her bag and handed it to Diana. In the confusion everyone's attention was either on the children or on Grinin; nobody was watching the Nanny.

Felicity tipped the vial of norovirus into Nanny's pocket and was away before anyone including Sokol saw her. Field agents were trained to do drops blindfolded and Ʊ7 had learned *that skill* thoroughly

3:00 p.m.
The Grinin's Penthouse, River Heights, S.W.1

*T*he day before Emma and Olga's birthday party, Sokol called Farringdon who was to act as a cook and live and sleep in the penthouse. Although he was only OhZone technical grade, he was competent and reliable and would always report to her as well as Blanka. She was after all ƲSecond-in-Command. There were plenty more OhZone techies. But she got a shock when she presented Farringdon at River Heights. Grinin seemed confused when he met them in the hall. He introduced the third MI5 security placement, Mick, already acting as cook and complementing the 24-hour team outside the building.
'See how popular I am,' Grinin laughed. 'Everyone wants to come and *live* with me!'
Grinin went on to say how pleased he was with his new cook. He had questioned him more about his culinary credentials than his security clearances and it transpired that Mick had learnt Russian cuisine during three tours of duty at the British Embassy in Moscow when on secondment to MI6.
'That settled it for me,' Grinin declared. 'I am surrounded by secu-

rity but a cook, a real cook! I couldn't be happier.'

Diana frowned at her husband and politely asked Sokol if she would like to stay for tea. With equal politeness Sokol declined and returned Farringdon to his duties in the back of the water company truck.

The next day, the day of Emma and Olga's birthday, Sokol arrived at 3 p.m., a full hour early. Emma ran into her arms but Olga was preoccupied with her tiger. 'I made her myself and look what she does.' She pressed the tiger's heart and a voice recording inside played Major Grinin's gruff voice

> *Come on Olga, come on Emma.*
> *Let's play the hiding game*

The hiding game was an elaborate Russian form of hide-and-seek which Major Grinin had invented. It not only incorporated Russian dolls and clues but also treats at different stages of the game. As Sokol, Diana, Grinin, officer Gabor and the children played the hiding game along with the toy tiger, the Nanny and MI5 Mick put the finishing touches to the food. As the various guests and their small children arrived they were regaled by a spectacular array of Russian cuisine and served Russian Caravan tea. No one from MI6 per se had been invited. Blanka had agreed with Grinin that to invite figures such as Russia, friendly to their cause, would compromise them. A birthday card had come however signed by Miss Banks and several at MI6, including Russia, Jude, Devices and Asia.

Blanka arrived with a present for both the children. They kissed her dutifully and rushed to tear open the beautiful blue wrapping paper. Blanka believed little girls should be free to wear blue, so the Kilburn Cosmonauts tiny-size Rugby shirts were the light blue of the team. Olga went quiet and wrapped her Rugby shirt around her toy tiger. Emma spent the rest of the party wearing the blue football shirt on top of her party dress. 'It's just for today,' laughed Diana to Blanka. 'Maybe it will be an emerald green one soon,' she whispered. Blanka winked back.

But for the twins the hit of the party was Nearby's arrival dressed in a Russian 19th century ball gown. She rarely dressed up but for this particular occasion she decided to put the boat out. It was mainly to amuse the twins, but she thought that Diana and Grinin would like it too. The historical ball gown was not hard to obtain: she spoke perfect Russian and worked for MI6. Painting her nails silver with gold bits on was – well, most *unusual*. Everyone was surprised, and stunned by her appearance.

Grinin feigned to not know who she was, and pretended she had arrived through a time warp. *Ra Ra Rasputin* was put on and Grinin lead circle dancing around the aquarium. Nearby held his one hand and Diana held his ass.

Emma and Olga thought the best fun was to ride along the Turkish carpets using the tails of Nearby's dress as a vehicle. The grandest carpet was between the aquarium and Grinin's desk by the window. 'It's a magic carpet,' shrieked Emma excitedly.

Olga turned to her toy tiger and asked. 'Is it?' She moved the tiger so it could whisper in her ear, and listened. Olga nodded her head, then turned and pronounced to everyone: 'It's a *secret* carpet.'

'Yes,' whispered Grinin, confidentially to her and Emma, as the lights were switched off for them to blow out the six candles on their birthday cake (which was shaped like the continents of the world). 'It's a *secret carpet!*' With a *whoosh* he raised his arm dramatically to the ceiling. The light of the tropical fish aquarium angled on his chiselled and bearded face. 'That,' he said, 'Is even better than magic.'   ℧

Für das Kind

Tuesday. 6.20 a.m.
Bio's apartment, S.W.1

*F*elicity sat up in bed with Bio still asleep beside her. She stared at the closed curtains of Bio's luxurious bedroom as, outside, an overcast morning numbly declared itself.

The UK is the only country where civil servants enjoy pensions worth more than 100 percent of their final salary [source: OECD, organisation for economic co-operation and development]. As the youngest director of MI6, Bio enjoyed salary, tax-free 'allowances' and pension package the envy of any CEO. She also enjoyed the perks. One of the perks was about to bite her nipple.
Bio groaned in her sleep, 'It's too early' and rolled away.

The curtains were blue with a pattern of anonymous flowers. A style her orphan children might draw, thought Felicity. Emma and Olga even.

What a bear of a man and yet his twins are so fragile, such tiny angels. And his wife, so young, smothered under that huge rough old man. Fucking him must be painful. No gentleness in him. Loud and brutish. And yet that produced two angels.

Felicity grabbed Bio's hair and jerked her head back. 'It's never too early when I'm awake. Do you want me to drag you out of bed? Soak your head under cold water?'

'You're not strong enough,' Bio retorted then, remembering Felicity's week-old OhZone-hood, regretted it.

'Do you want to rephrase that?' Felicity said, tossing Bio over her shoulder and carrying her to the bathroom.

Felicity sat on the rim of the tub, with Bio's face buried between her thighs, and roughly shampooed her. When she was finished she pulled Bio's head back and smiled with a cold detached look in her brown eyes.

Back in the bedroom, as Felicity dried Bio's hair with a plain white terry-cloth towel, Bio suddenly grabbed her hand.

'What are you thinking about?' she asked in what, Felicity decided, was a rather pathetic tone.

'About all the ways I can hurt you.'

'Don't. I was serious.'

'Didn't you hurt her? The Nanny?' Felicity asked coyly.

'I was quite proper and affectionate. Caught up in the rush of emotion.'

'The rush of emotion. I like that. You must show me sometime. Did she like the little-black-dress?'

'Yes.'

'And she'll be wearing it tomorrow?'

'She wanted to wear it today, but I told her we'd meet for dinner tomorrow after work if she wore it then,' Bio said as she grabbed Felicity and pulled her back on the bed.

Once they were finished playing, Felicity pulled a pantsuit from a Samsonite bag. In the bottom was another little-black-dress with a Harrod's tag still on it. She touched it and for a moment let herself imagine Grinin's large bear hands pressed against the flimsy dress and her body tight and resisting beneath the fabric

The London Eye, South Bank, S.W.1

Seated high in a compartment on the Eye, disguised as a workman, Felicity contemplated River Heights on the other bank of the river. It was eight stories high and the building to the left of it (the original *Scotland Yard*) was covered in scaffolding. She checked her iPhone then focussed her binoculars on the building to the right. The Old Cabinet Office building was destined, in two years time, to be the 'New' New-Scotland-Yard. But the Met police weren't in it yet. She had persuaded Frank Ryder to give her all sorts of access to it. He had been most obliging.

Grinin planned to celebrate his wedding anniversary by going on the Eye with his family at nine thirty. They had booked seats. Using her powers of persuasion, Felicity had arranged with Luke, the charge hand, to allow her to have continuous turns. She'd known Luke for over a year; they were fuckbuddies, so it wasn't hard. One of the MI5 protection team was standing under the Eye, but he hadn't a clue that the workman above him was Felicity. She checked her iPhone. The time was 08:59. With her compact military binoculars she watched Diana step out of the revolving door holding the hands of Emma and Olga. Officer Gabor nodded to her. Grinin followed and crossed the road. He stood there breathing in the river air. Central London's gold medal NO_2 pollution [stunting childrens' growth and increasing the risk of asthma and lung cancer] had yet to kick in. Grinin's timing, like hers, was impeccable, thought Felicity, as Big Ben started to strike the hour.

She watched the MI5 Woman and her own husband, Jude, attach

themselves to the procession, as the Grinin family passed Boudica's statue and turned left onto Westminster Bridge. Jude was good in bed but he didn't really turn her on: he was far, far too 'nice'. She imagined sex in bed with this bear, Rasputin. Diana's only five years older than me, she thought, as she flipped the binoculars on to Diana's smiling face – and he keeps her well satisfied by the look of it.

As everybody's attention was on the Grinin procession, a red Range Rover pulled up at the bottom of the steps to River Heights. The rental car man handed the keys to Frank Ryder, who drove the Range Rover into the private garage beneath the building.

By the time Felicity swung her binoculars back, to focus on who was watching Grinin, the car had gone. The Russians had a small group of would-be tourists on Victoria Embankment as well as the black SUV further up the road. Felicity could have tipped off MI5 about them but that wasn't her job. OhZone had another water company truck by a cordoned off manhole. Felicity momentarily pitied the agent assigned to help OhZone check London's sewers. She knew from personal experience how terrible they were. Probably no other English woman had walked as many miles of the London sewer system as she had. She checked the ℧Scanner and picked up the signals from inside the main water company truck at the rear of River Heights where Hans and Farringdon were watching the security cameras. Turning her attention back to Grinin as he approached the South Bank with his entourage, she thought about him and Diana again. It's their wedding anniversary, have they had sex this morning? Grinin kept the cameras and bugs permanently disabled in his bedroom so there was no record of how often he and Diana fucked. How often was it? He was a bear of a man, probably huge. Her iPhone beeped. She clicked on the message from C, and winced. It read

317885

8.3

7.00 p.m.
10 Downing Street, S.W.1

*A*fter his slot on BBC Radio 2 on Monday, Grinin had rung L.B.J. asking to meet the Prime Minister. Mr Corduroy was thrilled, and only twenty-four hours later Grinin was driven to Horse Guards and sneaked into Number 10 through a rear door. Officer Gabor, the MI5 Woman and Paddington sat in an ante room while Grinin and Mr Corduroy discussed the arts in general, and opera in particular, over Russian tea.

'Do you know Michael Marians, chief firearms officer at MI6?' Jermaine asked. 'He's very big in amateur operatics. You might know him as *Arms...*' he faltered, his eyes falling on Grinin's stump.

'Is this a dagger which I see before me?' said Grinin, right on cue. Blanka had primed him that the P.M. was keen for the security services to put on a production of Verdi's opera *Macbeth*. 'To keep their minds focussed on *service* rather than *plotting*,' Corduroy had said to one of Blanka's friends high in the Met police.

'Talking of the Scottish Play,' Grinin said casually, 'I wonder, as we approach the centenary of my namesake's torture, castration and murder, at the hands of MI6, whether you would now make an official apology to Russia?'

Mr Corduroy seemed surprised and confused. 'MI6?' he said to one of his aides. The aide nodded. 'Rasputin? Like your theme song? he said to Grinin.

'Yes,' repeated Grinin. 'Grigori Rasputin. It's been ninety-nine years but an apology would be nice.' The aide was shaking his head.

'I don't have *all* the facts,' the P.M. said. 'But I'll certainly look into it.'

8.4

Wednesday, March 18. 9:50 a.m.
River Heights, S.W.1

*B*y those who actually do it, creative work is generally considered to be ten percent inspiration and ninety percent perspiration. In MI6, Intelligence work was said to be sixty-nine percent exploration, thirty percent exasperation and one percent expiration. So the next day, when a Royal Navy gunboat unexpectedly appeared at the river landing, it was a welcome relief to Grinin's guards. It was probably innocent, but Paddington and the second MI5 officer went to check the gunboat's occupants. Then the Nanny left through the revolving door in her black leather jacket and little-black-dress. Not on the schedule, thought the Special Branch officer, about to end his early-hours shift. Well, one person less to watch. The Nanny looked pale but she nodded as she descended the steps. The MI5 Woman on the street wondered, is she in a hurry to see someone?

Once out of sight of the MI5 Woman, the Nanny grabbed a paper bag from her purse and threw up in it as discreetly as she could. Taking a deep breath and dabbing her mouth with a handkerchief, she paused to re-orient herself. Then, with more than usual determination, she walked towards Big Ben, dropped the bag into a litter bin and descended into Westminster Underground station. The MI5 Woman radioed to Mick inside Grinin's penthouse. 'The Nanny's gone into the tube, she's heading for home.'
'Yeah, she's feeling a bit sick,' came the reply over her radio. 'More than a bit, I'd say,' the MI5 Woman suggested.

Down Victoria Embankment, Lara yawned in the back of the black SUV. Her sergeant turned to her and said, 'The nanny's gone home.' Lara nodded. This is going to be a long stake out, she thought. She still hadn't decided what to do when Grinin drove off to Ireland. She was only certain of one thing: the KGB was the only agency that knew of his plan. She had a car on standby, she'd had Irish plates put on it. What would happen when the ferry reached Dublin? The Irish 'G2' were outside the cozy '5 Eyes' Intelligence agreement between the other English-speaking nations, but would they help her? What if they were smarter than the Brits?

'Anything new?' Crusoe asked as he climbed into the back of the water company truck at the rear of River Heights. He was there to relieve Krishna. 'Diana went to work an hour ago,' answered Krishna, putting on his coat. 'Grinin's been blasting out Tchaikovsky and Russian disco groove so loud it made the Nanny sick and she's gone home. Blanka's kidney is acting up. She's going to hospital for tests.'

'Not good. Where's Farringdon?' asked Crusoe.

'Being sick behind some bushes,' answered Krishna. 'Hans is down with it too. He better be okay by tomorrow, he's off to become one of you OhZones,' Krishna said.

'It's been put back, he's staying on the Op,' said Crusoe, waving.

'Good. Mind how you go,' said Krishna as he disappeared out the door.

In the shadow of Big Ben, the Nanny re-emerged from Westminster subway station. She blinked, put her bag over the shoulder of her leather jacket and walked back towards River Heights.

Crusoe watched her carefully on the monitors. As Farringdon climbed into the back of the truck, Crusoe said, 'The Nanny's back.'

'Probably forgot something,' Farringdon replied. He called on the ʊScanner, 'Nanny's back.'

'Copy that,' came Nearby's voice from the CIA-Blue control. At the

same time the MI5 Woman called Mick. 'The Nanny's back.'
'Rapid recovery,' said Mick.
The Nanny walked up the steps to River Heights and nodded to
officer Gabor, who had just taken over. He raised his bushy eyebrows as she entered. Big Ben proceeded to chime its introduction
to the hour, followed by ten deep notes.

Inside the lounge of the penthouse a Deutsche Grammophon vinyl
record, *Pictures at the Exhibition*, spun on the transcription turn-
table. At his desk, Grinin sipped his black Russian Caravan tea and
moved his head to the sound of the Berlin Philharmonic Or-
chestra. He put the cup on the saucer and picked up his pen. A
fountain pen, with black ink. A single sheet of blue paper contained this note to Diana, in Russian

> I am doing what seems best – because I cannot fight MI6 any
> longer and continue to endanger your three lives.
> Six years ago, you found a cynical, broken and damaged man
> drinking himself to death in a Moscow bar. You transformed
> this Rasputin through your love – you made me anew.
> Everything that means anything to me now has been made
> possible through your love . I don't believe, in this care-torn
> world, that any two people could've been happier

The Nanny stepped out of the private key elevator into the long hall
of the penthouse. From the far end came the Russian music. In the
playroom just beside her the twins noisily raced the four-car Sca-
lectric set their parents had bought them for their birthday. The
Nanny closed the playroom door and was about to lock it, when
Mick in his chef's apron approached her. 'You're back. Are you
feeling better?'

'Yes, thank you,' the Nanny answered, hanging her jacket in its
usual place. Her iPhone tumbled out of her bag onto the carpet. As

Mick bent to pick it up, the Nanny injected him in the back of the neck with a 2ml tranquillizer syringe, covered his mouth with her hand and lowered him onto the floor. She picked up her bag, took out two more tranquillizer syringes and hid them on the hall table behind the Toby jug of Queen Elizabeth the Second.

Grinin felt something over his left shoulder and turned his head. As he gazed across the lounge the Nanny opened the door and walked in. Grinin patted his pockets: where were his glasses when he needed them? 'I thought you'd gone home, you had a virus,' he said in Russian. The Nanny looked at him and replied in Russian. He couldn't quite understand what she was saying. Grinin stood up and cut the music to background. 'I beg your pardon?' he said. 'Do you like my dress?' the woman asked in English.
The moment Grinin heard the voice, he knew the end game had come. Early.

As he looked at the record label spinning, he thought of all the records made since Deutsche Grammophon had started in 1898, of all the lives begun and lived out on this 'small spinning fragment of solar driftwood'. The fish seemed to sense his mood and several orange and red ones spun around, in their own particular way, and moved close to him. He reciprocated and spoke to them in Russian, ignoring the woman in the little-black-dress.
'*Tak zdes.* So here it is, dear ones, it has come to this.'
Here is death at morning tea-time, he thought, and sadly you must watch her do her work. Thank God I talked to Diana last night. She'll know what to do.

'Do you like my dress, Major?' The woman's voice persisted. 'I bought it specially for the occasion.'
Felicity closed the lounge door, locked it and placed the key in her purse.

'I was expecting you tomorrow,' Grinin said, smiling grimly. 'Could you come back?'

Felicity laughed. Her nipples were unbelievably erect. This was Rasputin as she had hoped him to be. 'But I'm here for you today,' she simpered.

Stalling for time, Grinin rubbed his beard. 'I take it you're the rogue OhZone 7.'

'Keep up old man,' answered Felicity. 'I'm the future of OhZone.'

'I'm not going to debate with you.'

'That's good,' said Felicity. 'I hate debates.'

'*Khorosho*. Get it over with,' he demanded. 'Haven't you got a gun or piano wire or a poisoned dart? Wonderland is especially good with undetectable poisons.' Felicity eyed him coldly.

'I've got presents for Olga and Emma,' she said.

A look of unease passed over Grinin's face.

Cocking her ear to the sound of the Scalextric, she asked, 'Were the racing cars a birthday present?'

The muscles in Grinin's face tensed and his lips stiffened. He slowly inched towards the aquarium.

This wasn't Felicity's first hit, but it was her first hit as an OhZone and her first hit wearing a prosthetic appliance. 'Do you mind if I slip it off?' she quipped, gesturing to her face. 'It's not really me.'

Grinin thought quickly: what does she want with the children? Re-think, buy time, make this her *last hit*. He swept his arm courteously in her direction, 'Be my guest.' As Felicity peeled the prosthetic face off, Grinin reached the edge of his aquarium. He could tell she was little better than an amateur. She wasn't paying attention and hadn't brought out her Sig. Instead she posed before him like a model on a runway, reached down to the hem of her dress and hiked it up showing bare thigh above her hold-up. 'What do you think?' she asked. He thought Felicity had the complexion of a vampire (what the Scots called 'blue' skin color) but Grinin raised his eyebrows and pursed his lips.

'Would you like to die fucking me?' asked Felicity. 'I could strangle you as you cum, and you're still hard inside me.'

Grinin almost laughed at her. But the grimness of the situation held him in check. What does she want with Emma and Olga?

He pointed at his fish. 'I would love to,' he said. 'Just let me feed my fishes dear, one last time. You wouldn't deny an old man a small pleasure, before such a *feast* of the senses.'

Felicity, now flushed, slipped off her shoes, lifted her left leg onto an antique chair and started to unroll her hold-up. Everyone knew Grinin was unarmed and had refused the KGB's weapons, Felicity assured herself. MI5 Mick was out for the count, and OhZone and all the others were locked out of the elevator system. She had twenty minutes before Blanka could get anyone into the penthouse. All the time in the world for riding his huge dick on the black leather sofa. The escape plan was perfect and the children were locked in their playroom, ready for her.

Felicity was trained to be super-observant, but she made her second mistake: she missed the CIA-Blue on the island inside the aquarium. Grinin had pressed the 'SOS' button, sending its silent alarm to the water company truck, the Blue control in Blanka's stable, the CIA bureau in Baker Street and probably the KGB too. My dear little-black-dress assassin, Grinin told himself, you might not have as long as you think.

As she set her bare leg on the carpet and the hold-up on the antique chair, Felicity remembered: bugger, the playroom door wasn't locked. A wave of frustration crossed her face and Grinin saw it.

*I*n the back of the water company truck Crusoe's cell phone read, 'Redialling...' He got another engaged tone from Gabor at the front door. Something was wrong, he had a bad feeling about the Nanny. He threw down his cell phone and called Blanka on the ℧Scanner, but there was just white noise. Something was very wrong. The truck door opened and Farringdon climbed back in. Crusoe tossed him the Scanner. 'What the hell's going on?' he asked.

'You mean apart from me throwing up,' Farrington said as he checked the Scanner on various frequencies on his equipment. 'We're being jammed,' he said. 'GCHQ are jamming the secure frequencies, and our cell phones. It just started.'

'Shit! It's the hit! Mayday to Blanka,' Crusoe ordered.
Farringdon hit a crimson button labeled

Public waveband S.O.S.

The button flashed red as it transmitted 'SOS' as a text from a series of unassigned cell numbers in the system. The CIA-Blue radio is missing, thought Crusoe. 'Find the Blue, where the hell's the Blue?' Farringdon swept coffee cups onto the floor, turned paper work upside down. 'It was right here.'
'Did anyone relieve you when you were sick? Was Krishna alone?'
'Prosthetics John stepped in to lend a hand – shit!'
Crusoe pulled open a closet, removed the sleek, non-Newtonian fluid OhZone body armor and zipped it around himself. It covered him as far as his knees.
'The elevator will be disabled,' he said.
Farringdon leapt out of the truck, pulled open a service hatch and pulled out a coil of hi-tech zip line, a carbon fibre cross bow with an ℧UVX sight on it, and a pneumatic bolt gun. A backup cell phone bought-for-cash rang on the monitors desk. Crusoe answered it as he secured the ℧Armor.

Over the noise of Blanka's Mini Cooper engine and siren, Crusoe could hear Blanka's voice with a kind of panic in it. 'We go under the barrier, duck!'
He was as clear as he could be: 'Felicity disguised as Nanny. Prosthetics John took our Blue. GCHQ's jamming us.'
'Copy that,' replied Nearby, 'Sokol five minutes in chopper. We're –'
There was the crash of Blanka's suspension grounding.
'–Through St James' Park, two minutes!'
'I'm going up the side, tell Blanka to take the elevator shaft,' Crusoe said, as he jumped out the truck door and ran with Farringdon and their gear to the foot of River Heights.

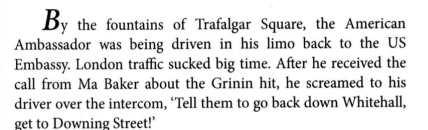

*B*y the fountains of Trafalgar Square, the American Ambassador was being driven in his limo back to the US Embassy. London traffic sucked big time. After he received the call from Ma Baker about the Grinin hit, he screamed to his driver over the intercom, 'Tell them to go back down Whitehall, get to Downing Street!'

At the CIA London bureau, Ma Baker cursed the fact his helicopter was picking up the CIA Director at Heathrow. Admiral De Leon could not have come at a worse time. Twelve agents with siege kits scrambled into three vans; two trying the Park Lane route, one headed for Regent's Street, Trafalgar Square and then River Heights. Ma Baker made one call to the Embassy. Another two cars and four agents started on the shorter fifteen minute journey to River Heights: less than ten if they ran red lights and one-way streets as he'd told them to.

*G*rinin looked at Felicity's legs (one with black hold-up, one bare) and then at the other hold-up on his 18th century chair. 'My Nanny wears proper stockings-with-garters, not those cheap things from Marks and Spencer,' he said.

Felicity didn't believe her ears. Was this a seventy-five year old putting down a late-twenties beauty who wanted to fuck him?

'*What* did you say?'

'You heard me,' replied Grinin.

Felicity decided she wouldn't fuck him, she'd just kill him.

She'd missed the CIA-Blue in the aquarium so when Grinin had removed a World War Two British Enfield No 2 revolver [made in the same year, 1940, as Grinin himself] from a tin of fish-treats, it went unnoticed too – until he whipped it from the pocket of his ornate housecoat and pointed it at her chest. Felicity hadn't worn a holster for her Sig in case it spoilt her figure. For the same reason she had broken an OhZone golden rule and not worn her ʊ Armor. It matched the dress but she would've had to wear a three-sizes-bigger-black-dress. That would never do. If Grinin had been wearing his glasses he would have noticed Felicity's erect nipples, betraying her complete absence of body armor! Within the KGB he'd been classed as 'marksman first class' and he *was left-handed*, so – in the time it took Felicity to remove the Sig 321 from her bag – he raised the barrel and fired two shots at her head.

One round just missed her neck, hitting the wall. The other .38/200 bullet whistled past her cheek and clipped the tip of her left ear. As she instinctively yowled and clutched it, blood trickled down her cheek and neck and onto the little-black-dress. The shock knocked Felicity off balance and she slipped on the grandest Turkish carpet – Olga's *secret* carpet – and crashed to the floor, sending her 321 sprawling across the room to the desk.

His neighbours in River Heights were used to Grinin playing the *1812 Overture*, he was considerate about when he did it and a model neighbour in every other respect. Mrs Townshend in the apartment below took pains to explain this as she called the emergency services and spoke to the Met police. 'But what I heard sounded more like gun shots than musical canon fire,' she insisted.

Without his glasses Felicity's head was too small a target, thought Grinin, so as she jumped nimbly to her feet, he fired at the flash of white flesh above her right knee. The round-nosed slug keyholed, making a surprisingly large wound for a small calibre. Felicity stumbled and he shot her through the foot for good measure.

As Felicity gasped and looked down at the blood pouring from her leg, Grinin seized the moment, strode forward and pulled the trigger eighteen inches from her head. But the trusty Enfield finally jammed. In a stunt no one would have thought a one-armed-Rasputin capable of, Grinin dropped the Enfield, rolled over the carpet and seized Felicity's Sig. This state-of-the-art pistol would have a dozen rounds in it. He cocked it but when he pulled the trigger all the Sig did was click and beep. He pulled the trigger again and the same thing happened. Felicity smiled and held out her hand for it.

It was a rig Blanka had designed for the OhZone 321s: the gun was handprint activated and would not fire for anyone's hand but ʊ7. For the only time in her life Felicity was grateful to Blanka. The forty-five depleted uranium round would have gone straight through her (even if she'd been wearing ʊArmor) and then on and out the side of the building.

Through the panoramic window behind Grinin, Felicity saw a distress rocket (fired into the air by Farringdon) burst into a shower of red over the River Thames. Her face showed fear for the first time. Grinin hurled the 321 at her nose, but her reactions were lightning quick and she caught it.

With five strides and one kick from her uninjured leg, she broke

Grinin's jaw. As he lay on the floor, she kicked him with all her OhZone might sending him crashing into the wall where he writhed in pain.

Kicking his legs apart, pinning them and aiming her Sig, she said, 'I will have *that* one way or another.'
She pulled the trigger. The 321 clicked and beeped. 'Bugger!' she yelled. She looked down the ʊSight and saw the message

Handprint recognition paused

and a seconds counter winding down from forty-six. Felicity regretted leaving the OhZone training early [she had been bored in Paris]. Stuffing the gun in her bag she brought out a garrotte wire. She slipped it around the old man's neck effortlessly and turned the wooden pegs.

Grinin gasped, tried to cough, and started to turn red then purple behind his beard. He struggled to his feet bravely, his massive body tossing Felicity about and covering his face and housecoat with the blood running from her leg. But he was no match for a young fit OhZone, even a wounded one. Felicity clung to him and tightened the garrotte in the prescribed way.

Grinin's face slowly started to turn gray. With Felicity's weight on his back, he was brought down like a big-game-animal. She held the garrotte tight as he made his last struggle for life, blood gurgling from his mouth and soaking his beard. Then, silent and still, his grotesquely twisted face coughed no more.

Felicity undid the bloody wire, wiped it on a tissue from her bag and slipped it out of sight. As a final touch she lifted Grinin (her OhZone strength made it easy) and carried him over to the aquarium. With a heave she dumped his body face down over the glass and into the tank. He plunged to the bottom of the tropical water in a swell of bubbles and bloody froth with the alarmed fish swimming around him. Grinin's body then bobbed back up to the surface, face up. A couple of bolder fish started to investigate his flesh.

'You did want to feed your "fishes dear," one last time,' she mocked.

Felicity looked down into Grinin's dead brown eyes. Her mind flashed to Diana's blue eyes, and then to the twins' brown eyes. Were their eye-color alleles identical too? Soon she would be able to find out.

Compulsively, Felicity reached into the aquarium and felt Grinin's hair and beard. As she was about to touch his open eyes, the Sig in her handbag gave three beeps and came back to life. She froze. A strange sensation overcame her: those eyes, could he still look at her, see her? She didn't believe in reincarnation but she did believe in spooky weird shit happening so, turning away, Felicity grabbed Grinin's one arm and flipped his body over so that it was face down in the water again. She didn't want *him* coming back to life on her.

Felicity turned her back on the sea of red, Grinin's body a grotesque whale amid scurrying fish. Behind her, Grinin's cell phone started ringing. She ignored it, took her purse from her bag and the key from her purse. On Grinin's phone the caller ID said

Diana

The blood from Felicity's wounds made bizarre modern art out of the Turkish pattern on the 'secret carpet.' She smudged the blood with her big toe. Not to my taste, thought Felicity. Give me Monet any day, and he painted a lot of water scenes. She limped to the hall door, unlocked and opened it, and looked past the antique table towards the elevator and unconscious Mick. She reached into her bag, took out an MI6 forensic pouch and removed the Emma and

Olga badges. Then she produced another and took out two paper bags of American candy from the orphans' carnival. 'For the children,' Felicity said aloud. 'My little brown-eyed *Zwilingers*.'

Holding her fine-featured head high – despite the bloodied side of her face, still the cat with the cream – she started to stride into the hall, the pain from the bullet wounds in her leg and foot making her wince. Sensing something behind her, Felicity glanced over her shoulder into the lounge. The intercom in the hall buzzed loudly.

'Emma, Olga!,' a voice shouted over the intercom, 'This is Blanka. Run and hide!' Looking towards the hall in panic, Felicity crashed into the antique table. The Toby jug of the Queen toppled to the floor and smashed into pieces, while the tranquillizer syringes landed softly amidst the jagged pieces.

Another voice came over the intercom, more restrained. 'Emma, Olga, this is Nearby. The woman in the apartment is not your Nanny. She's got a gun and wants to hurt you. Barricade your bedroom. Don't let her in.'

Who let the Queen Bitches in? thought Felicity. 'I'll see you in hell,' she hissed into the intercom, ripping it out of the wall.

O Reader, here the writer of this story must pause. She hesitates to turn the page. But History does not stop or turn away, not even when the heart is breaking   ℧

A list of writers whose works have been cited in this book (where credit is not given on the page). These are either used with permission; or are used for purposes described in the laws of various countries for fair usage / fair dealing such as the US Copyright Law (Title 17) Section 107 and the UK Copyright Designs and Patents Act Section 28 onwards; or copyright has expired. No writer's work is cited or used with the intention of breaching copyright.

(This list is being completed as of April 2017)

p6 The Sirens of Titan by Kurt Vonnegut Jr. Victor Gollancz, 1962

p13 Where To Now St Peter by Elton John & Bernie Taupin published by
    Universal Music Publishing Group, used by permission.

p15/17 She's Not There by Rod Argent, used by permission.

[7] from 'This Way For The Gas Ladies & Gentlemen' by Tadeusz Borowski
    translated by Ralph Ralph (1990) London: Penguin Books

Raechel Sands is represented by Nancy Owen Barton Agency - nowenb@aol.com

Raechel Sands asserts the moral right to be identified as the author of this work